To Archie
kind regards
Paul

Ghost Train

And other Tales of the Unsuspecting

An anthology of past, present and future short stories

Fiction by Paul R Goddard published by Clinical Press Ltd.
(Paperback and/or ebook form)

The characters in some of the short stories also appear in other books by Paul R Goddard.

Thrillers:
The Sacrifice Game: El Juego del Sacrificio
- The Confessions of Saul
- The Writing on the Wall
- Reincarnation
- The Fellowship of the Egg (to be published late 2015)

Fantasy:
The fantasy books all inter-relate but are separate complete stories
The Witch, the Dragon and the Angel Trilogy

- Witch Way Home?
- Witch Armageddon?
- Witch Schism and Chaos?

plus two more (it's a magical trilogy!)
- Tsunami
- Change

and a prequel
- Parsifal's Pact

The Witches' Brew Trilogy:

- Hubble Bubble
- Toil
- Trouble

On a similar theme
- Oberon's Bane

An Anthology of Fantasy and Science Fiction Poetry
- Parables from Parallel Places:

Ghost Train

And other Tales of the Unsuspecting

An anthology of past, present and future short stories

Paul R Goddard
© 2015

First published in the UK (as an anthology) 2015

ISBN   978-1-85457-080-2

Published by: Clinical Press Ltd., Redland Green Farm, Redland, Bristol, BS6 7HF, UK.

CONTENTS

Introduction

Short stories, poetry and song lyrics have a lot in common. They are stories that take up a very few number of words compared with their big brother the novel. In a twelve bar blues the story has to be accomplished in just twelve bars or six lines, the first two of which are repeated. Here is a simple example penned myself.

> *I love you baby*
> *Listen now to my beat*
> *I love you baby*
> *Listen now to my beat*
> *Why don't you love me?*
> *Is it 'cos of my smelly feet?*

That amusing song tells a whole story. The singer is in love, but the object of his desire is not so enamoured despite the lover's beating heart or perhaps musical prowess. The lover wonders if the cause is the peculiar odour emanating from the area below his legs but the answer is not forthcoming.

Poems are similar but can be considerably longer....that is if you don't want people to read them!

Short stories vary from perhaps just a few hundred words of Flash Fiction to several thousand words. Novellas are longer at 20,00 to 60,000 and novels overlap ranging from 50,000 words up into the millions.

I have written a separate anthology of poetry and, so far, have had thirteen novels published ranging from 50,000 to 100,000 words. They have achieved some popularity but mostly as e-book free downloads. It is, of course, always a lot easier to give things away than it is to sell them.

Over the Yuletide period 2014 I had three number ones in the Amazon download of e-books worldwide rankings and two books that came in second. The number one hits were *Reincarnation* which reached the top spot in Financial thrillers (Amazon free downloads worldwide) keeping another of my books, *The Writing on the Wall* at number two. *Oberon's Bane*, an exciting fantasy mixed with science fiction, was Number 1 in the Celtic, English and Welsh Myths and Legends category, whilst *Parables from Parallel Places* reached the same prime position in Poetry anthologies and was No 2 of the Love poems for all the days it was available free.

Witch Way Home? had previously squeezed into the top ten free science fiction downloads on Amazon worldwide (Witch Way Home, number 9 in sci fi on October 31st 2014).

In this anthology of short stories there is a little poetry but only when I can't resist the opportunity. The stories do vary in length whilst still keeping true to the genre.

The content? You'll have to read them to find out but they are basically flights of fancy and imagination. Those ostensibly set in the past or present could have happened but, unless I have indicated otherwise, did not. The future stories are fantasy, straying into a variety of parallel worlds where science has developed frighteningly and magic has invaded the reality.

We start, of course, with the past...

Sherlock Holmes
And the Case of the Metrodolvian Princess

It was in the late Summer of '89 that Sherlock and I first encountered the evil creature who was later so well-known to the World as both Doctor Parthistle and the Surgical Snake. As Sherlock had remarked on a number of occasions, when a medical doctor is intent on evil they are the worst of the criminals. As a doctor myself I am saddened to have to admit that Sherlock, with his finely tuned mind, was right. Once turned to criminality a doctor has the knowledge, the nerve and the opportunity to undertake the worst of crimes. The doctor would plague us for some years but the case I shall refer to now did not directly involve the evil medical man.

My newly-wed wife, Mary, had decided to spend the weekend with her parents and I was to visit Sherlock in the Baker Street lodgings. Having dismissed my last patient at the end of a fairly quiet Saturday morning list, I hastened by Hansom to the old rooms that we had shared in my bachelor days.

'Well, my good friend,' Sherlock greeted me. 'You have arrived just in time to join me on what may turn out to be a fascinating case. Do you have your notebook handy.... and your trusty service revolver?'

Providing the affirmative to both the questions I sat in my usual chair and Sherlock glanced at me with some amusement.

'Our client, a Mrs Buckley, should arrive in two minutes time. But before she arrives make yourself comfortable and stop worrying about your last patient. The lady is recovering well and the treatment was successful.'

'How can you possibly tell?' I expostulated. 'I'm used to your ways and your abilities. But your detecting skills surely cannot extend to knowledge of my patients when you haven't even seen them!'

He laughed in his usual carefree manner when a new case was about to commence and the boredom, from which he suffered so cruelly, was about to be assuaged.

'I have observed in the past that the leather binding of your old family bible is decaying. I have, myself, written a short thesis on the subject of the twenty-three different moulds to be found on ancient leather. The type of mould on your bible temporarily stains the skin and I have observed such colouration on your own fingers.... and a slight stain of cosmetics on your cuff.'

I glanced at my right hand and concurred with his acute observation.

Sherlock continued. 'You came here in some haste at the end of your surgery list for you had not washed your hands. I know that you scrupulously wash your hands before you see each patient. Thus the staining must have occurred during or after the last patient that you saw. Now why should you pick up your family bible when you are rushing out to see me? It is much more likely that you would do so whilst the patient was still there.'

I looked at him with amazement for he was, as usual, quite right.

'And you will no doubt recall that you recently gave me a copy of your latest research paper: *The treatment of ganglion cysts with sharp compression.* As I recall the sharp compression you advised was to hit the ganglion with a family bible. With simple deduction I knew that your last patient had a ganglion cyst and that you delivered your prescribed treatment with the self-same bible.'

'But how do you know she is doing well?' I interjected

'Simple enough, dear Watson. In your short paper you had collected the results from 25 patients treated in that manner and all had done well. If there had been any complications you would have stayed and watched the patient. You did not do so, but came over to see me. By the laws of statistics I can reassure you that this patient will also do well, just like your 25 former patients with ganglion cysts. I know that you worry about your patients but this is one that should not disturb you.'

As I sat in wonderment at Holmes amazingly logical and clear mind I heard the faint ring of the bell announcing the arrival of the next client. Within a minute Sherlock's page, young Billy, showed the person in.

Not good-looking, she was a singular character of a uncertain age, quite large and wearing an eclectic choice of clothes. It was a warm day but she had a scarf muffled around her face and had on a large black cloak. This she took off with a shrug and she sat down where the great detective indicated, panting slightly. The woman had considerable layers of foundation giving her face a pallid appearance.

'You have received my letter?' she started to query in a very soft voice.

'Of course,' replied Sherlock. 'Or we would not have been expecting you as we clearly were. You made little or no indication in your letter as to why you wished to see me. However, it is apparently of some importance on a subject of some delicacy. You believed that you may be observed coming here and so wore the muffling clothes on a hot day. I feel bound to point out that doing so only made you more obvious.'

The client sighed at the implied criticism and shifted in the chair, clearly a little uncomfortable, but Sherlock was unstoppable.

'Your epistle made no reference to your address. But you live just outside Guildford and had to wait for you husband to go out before you came to see us. Your husband is in the civil service and you believe the problem in question may be of national significance. And you should really be called Lady Buckley, not Mrs. Buckley as in your letter.'

The lady now stared at the great detective in amazement.

'But how do you know all this?' she gasped, still speaking hoarsely. 'Have we met before? I don't remember such a meeting.'

Holmes laughed in his usual amused manner

'The combination of red mud and chalk seen on your shoes is most common just outside the Guildford area. You took a trap to Guildford station and caught the 10.15 express to London, thence you travelled by Tube to Baker Street and hastened to this appointment arriving here only just on time and somewhat out of breath. I presume that you could not leave to catch an earlier train, despite wishing to be punctual, and at your certain age you would only require to wait because a spouse may be in attendance. Your husband left for work and you came to see us. It took ten minutes to get to Guildford station, am I not right?'

The lady nodded and Holmes continued..

'So your husband left just before ten. You are from a very respectable upper middle class family and your husband is therefore a professional. But most professionals, working on a Saturday, would be at work by at least 9.00 am. One section of professionals are rather more tardy. The civil service. A small branch of the civil service was secretly moved down to the Guildford area just last year. This is the espionage section of the Department of Defence. Anything that is related to the Department of Defence is of national significance. Cogito ergo sum.'

The lady took a large breath and started her narrative.

'We have been married for eleven happy years. Our only regret until recently has been my inability to provide an heir for my husband. Ten months ago we moved from Belgravia to a large house just outside Guildford.'

I started with some surprise even though I should have known the unerring accuracy of the detective's observations.

'Your colleague was completely right,' said the lady looking towards me. 'My husband is a senior civil servant and I fear that he may have lost something of national importance.'

Sherlock raised one eyebrow in anticipation of what was to come next.

'And you, dear lady, fear that you were the cause of the loss?'

he suggested.

With a half sob she agreed that it was the case.

'And it was by accident,' I added, assuming that to be the case.

'No, no,' she replied shaking her head, 'Quite the opposite. I gave the object away on purpose. I did it to spite my husband but I did not realise its significance.'

'He was paying the object too much attention, I presume,' deduced Holmes. 'And the object in question was a portrait of a young lady.'

'But how could you possibly know?' Lady Buckley shook her head in amazement, repeating her astonishment at my friend's amazing powers of deduction.

'Elementary,' replied the sleuth. 'What other object would arouse the indignation of such a lady as yourself? But fear not. We can retrieve the painting of the Crown Princess of Metrodolvia.'

Lady Buckley rose in indignation.

'I did not tell you the name of the person in the portrait. Someone must have forewarned you of this event,' she exclaimed indignantly, retrieving her large feathered hat as she said this. 'You have been playing me along like a fool and I believed you. Fi to you and humbug.'

'Please seat yourself,' interjected Holmes calmly. 'Nothing could be further from the truth. It is simply that I have studied eclectically and one area of my research has been the monarchy of the smaller principalities.....'

Somewhat mollified Lady Buckley returned to her seat and Holmes continued.

'....And there is but one portrait that would hold the significance you have implied of this object. It is the portrait of the Metrodolvian Princess. The portrait which is the proof that she has the right to the throne. The portrait which shows her royal birthmark and demonstrates her legitimacy.'

The lady looked on in awe.

'Amazing Holmes! Just amazing!' I cried.

'Not quite as amazing as this,' cried Holmes reaching out and pulling off the lady's wig. 'Not quite the lady are we, Moriarty?'

'Curse you meddler,' shouted Holmes' greatest rival, his act revealed to an astonished Billy and an equally amazed biographer, namely myself.

Moriarty ran towards the door and I started forward, pulling my revolver out of my pocket.

'Let him go,' commanded Holmes, quietly.

'But why?' I asked in further bewilderment as the man clattered down the stairs and past an equally incredulous Mrs. Hudson. 'He is the arch criminal you have been trying to best.'

'Professor Moriarty is indeed such a person,' replied Sherlock.

'The Napoleon of crime, the organizer of half that is evil. That's what you called Moriarty,' I exhaled loudly.

Why was Sherlock letting the man escape?

'But that was not Professor Moriarty,' replied Sherlock.

'You said that it was!' I protested.

'Au contraire!' laughed Sherlock. 'That was Jim or James Moriarty, the Professor's younger brother.'

'Younger brother?'

'Yes indeed,' chuckled the detective. 'The professor is much older.'

'How did you realise that it was not the lady from the letter?'

'I thought that you would have noticed the broadness of his

shoes,' replied Holmes. 'And the very faint stubble under the layers of cosmetics. That much was obvious.'

'But the voice should have been a giveaway,' I protested.

'Never more than a whisper.'

'Even still I could have caught him,' I remarked ruefully.

'And so doing committed a crime for which we both may have been arrested,' replied the great detective. 'I have no proof that Jim Moriarty has ever been implicated in his brother's crimes.'

'So why did he come round today trying to fool us?' I asked.

'He was sent by his brother, of course,' stated Sherlock.

'Why would he do such a thing?' I was still terribly confused. 'Was it just a prank?'

'A prank? No, no. Far more than that,' grinned the detective, the fingers of both his hands pressed against each other like a man in prayer. 'But a game, certainly.'

'Go on, explain,' I was just a little exasperated.

'If we discovered Jim Moriarty's deception we risked apprehending him. We would then have been sued for assault since wasting our time and dressing as a woman is not yet illegal in our enlightened country,' stated Holmes.

'And if we did not discover that James Moriarty was acting the part of Lady Buckley?' I queried.

'I may have blundered into a web of deceit and tried to recover the painting from its rightful owner, thus setting off the very train of events that Professor Moriarty wanted to occur.'

'The Crown Princess of Metrodolvia really does have such a painting as proof of her right to the throne?'

'Yes and no,' replied Sherlock.

'What does that mean?' I was even more frustrated.

'The painting exists but it is presently not in her possession,' replied Sherlock. 'And Professor Moriarty was rather keen that I should believe in his brother's impersonation.'

'Why so?' I asked.

'To have gone to all that trouble with the mud on the shoes and the carefully constructed letter?' answered Sherlock, surprised that I had not followed his reasoning. 'And sending his brother, a man who was unsullied by crime but is, I understand and you will now agree, a great amateur actor.'

'Why would he go to that trouble?'

'He wanted me to recover the painting so that he, Professor Moriarty, would have control of it.'

'But how do you know that the painting is not in the possession of the Princess?' I asked. This was a step too far in the logic.

'Because I have it,' replied Sherlock. 'It was given to me for safe keeping by my brother Mycroft.'

'Why did he have it?' I queried.

'The lady in question gave it to him,' answered Holmes. 'It is, after all, the British Government and our Head of State, the Empress, who decide whether or not the royalty of Europe are who they say they are.'

'Is it?' I was once more amazed.

'Who else?' asked the great detective. 'Would you trust the Prussians, the Russians or the French?'

'Well no, obviously not. But surely the countries themselves make their own decisions.'

'As to who their royalty are?' Holmes laughed long and hard. 'You don't really believe that?'

'It would seem only fair,' I started.

'But the world is not fair and the Princess wishes to marry.'

'And that is the business of Queen Victoria and her government?' I was indignant.

'She wishes to marry one of Victoria's cousins. A certain Crown Prince, so I believe.'

'And we are protecting the painting so that this can happen?'

'Quite the opposite. It is the government's opinion that she only wishes to marry in order to create a powerful union of countries, which is certainly against the interest of the United Kingdom.'

'And is that your opinion?'

'That is something I have not decided as yet,' replied the consulting detective.

'And why did Mycroft give it to you?' I asked.

'Perhaps so that I could make the decision and not him, I suspect,' replied Sherlock Holmes, pensively.

'What is this painting like and where is it right now?' I asked.

'It is relatively small, twelve inches by nine in its frame, and on a piece of wood,' replied Holmes.

'So you put it in the safe?' I queried.

'That would be the first place that thief would look and we have had several break-ins,' replied Sherlock.

'So where did you put it?' I asked.

'That's the ironic bit,' answered the great detective. 'It's over there.'

He pointed to the very chair that Jim Moriarty had been sitting in.

'It's behind the cover,' explained Holmes. 'Against the back of the chair. I had just stowed it there when you arrived then Jim Moriarty appeared and sat back against it. The painting was the very reason that he could not make himself comfortable.'

Postscript

It is a matter of history that the Crown Princess did marry the Crown Prince of her choice. Sherlock made the decision to return the painting to its rightful owner and it is one of the reasons that the country concerned joined us with the Entente Powers or Allies against the Central Powers in the Great War. As usual Sherlock Holmes was proven to be correct in his conclusion which was probably reached by the most abstract of reasoning.

Doctor Parthistle, the Surgical Snake, will appear in a later memoir.

NOTE

Many writers have taken up the challenge of writing a Sherlock Holmes story. Conan Doyle, the originator, was himself a doctor and was inspired by Dr. Joseph Bell who he met at medical school. Bell's keen powers of observation impressed the medical student so much that he based his famous character, Sherlock Holmes, on his mentor.

The medical facts in the story are correct but please do not go around hitting people with bibles. This is not a textbook of medicine and there are now other treatments!

Holmes methods of analysis are further discussed in the next story

Holmes Chairs a Lecture

The hard winter of 1900 led into the cold spring of March 1901. Queen Victoria's long and eventful reign was at an end and it was the turn of her son Edward VII to take the realm at the head of the largest empire the world had ever known. I was busy with my practice and had for some time been absent from the eyrie in Baker Street in which resided the cleverest but also most frustrating man in the whole of Christendom. It was on a cold Tuesday late in March when I received a telegram indicating that I was needed at number 221B.

I finished my surgery and hastened to the great man's abode, the lodgings in which I had enjoyed so many happy hours but also endured hardship and fear.

To my surprise Sherlock Holmes was busy struggling with a particularly heavy dining room chair which he invited me to carry with him around to the local police station.

'Watson! I trust you have your service revolver?' enquired Holmes.

I nodded in reply and he continued.

'It is unlikely that there will be a problem but I am hoping for a few fireworks at my forthcoming lecture.'

'Lecture?' I queried the genius's statement.

I had never known Sherlock Holmes to give a public lecture though he had many times espoused in great detail the scientific method in criminal detection.

'I am giving a lecture on the importance of observation and method in police investigation,' smiled Holmes. 'And the chair is a case in point. I shall be describing upholstery and the method of reupholstering a damaged seat and I shall use it as an allegory for the science of detection.'

'Reupholstering a damaged seat?' I was completely bewildered. 'I thought that the peremptory summons to your aid might be to do with the Mayfair Ruby but a lecture on reupholstery? What is the relevance?'

I have to admit that I was more than a little irritated. I had plenty to do at the surgery and there were people waiting for me to visit them on my rounds. Now the missing ruby…that would have been worth the race across London.

'Elementary!' exclaimed Holmes with a sardonic grin. 'We peel away the layers of reality thus revealing the true nature of the chair, then put them back in order and our normality is resumed with the damage mended and the aberration corrected.'

I looked at him with astonishment. A chair as a method of detection? Whatever next? Was my genius friend losing the plot or was I becoming like the plodding policemen that Holmes would be lecturing to?

'I have written a small treatise on the subject and printed copies are already available at the police station. The audience will be small but learned, I believe,' stated Holmes.

'Lestrade?'

'Yes, our friend the Inspector will be there,' remarked Holmes. 'I am expecting several of the constabulary also.'

As we left the the apartment Holmes picked his deerstalker off the peg and placed it on his head. This was unusual. Ever since I had mentioned the hat in one of the published case histories Holmes had refused to wear the thing. I looked at him quizzically.

'On this occasion we must not disappoint the audience,' he replied, as ever reading my unasked question.

We entered the local headquarters of the Metropolitan Peelers and were ushered to a meeting room where rows of chairs had been set up. The audience numbered some twenty-five, of which there were just two women. About half of the people already sitting in the chairs were in uniform and they were mostly sat in the front rows. The other half had plain clothes and I was most surprised to see Mycroft amongst them. What could have attracted Sherlock's elder brother to such an occasion?

'Thank you for coming to my demonstration,' started Sherlock Holmes after he had been introduced by Lestrade. 'The good Inspector has, for some considerable time, been requesting that I should give a lecture on my methods of detection and, after deliberation, I was persuaded to take this opportunity.'

Lestrade nodded at his mention, assenting to the comment made by the great detective.

'You may consider it strange that I have brought a chair as the object of consideration but I am sure that the short treatise I have given you all on my simple methods and the comparison with the works of a furniture artisan will have explained why I am doing this. You will note that this chair, a fine solid article with a leather covered seat, has a small nick in the leather. I was lucky enough to purchase the chair at a considerably reduced price in the furniture emporium in Tottenham Court Road. This will be a theoretical lecture as well as a practical demonstration so I shall first talk about science in detection then we will have a break for afternoon tea, courtesy of the good inspector, followed by the practical. Whilst I am lecturing I would like everybody to take a look at this chair and make any notes about it that you may consider useful as if it were part of a criminal investigation, perhaps even something you might find at the scene of a crime. You may look at it during the break but do not touch it. I will then invite comments before resuming the lecture.'

Sherlock Holmes proceeded to give an excellent and erudite discourse on the nature of detection and observation emphasising the importance of deductive reasoning. I took copious notes, which I can barely read due to my poor writing skills probably resulting from a working lifetime writing too quickly as a doctor. I have distilled a few of the points below.

Number one: deduction is reasoning backwards. Most people if you describe a particular train of events can work out the result. They can put the events together in their mind and provide an answer. Such reasoning is commonplace but reasoning the other way round…from the result back to the train of events….now that is rare.

Number two: gather data before you theorise.

I am sure that this is where I, although a doctor and very familiar with the process of reasoning, have fallen down in the past. Despite his apparent wizardry at deduction Holmes had many times reminded me that first-hand evidence was the clay from which he made his bricks.

Number three: always notice trifles.

Number four: Avoidance of emotion.

That is about all I can read from my notes but I can add the following quote I recall from many of his cases: "When you have excluded the impossible, whatever remains, however improbable, must be the truth."

The policemen in the front row were the most conscientious at taking notes and I wish I could see some of their efforts now. We stopped for tea and filed into the next room. A few policemen stayed for a moment or two to examine the chair but eventually everybody enjoyed the convivial company of the tea party in the staff room of the police station. Lestrade had apparently purchased the cakes and I was amazed to witness such generosity on his part.

'Get stuck in doctor,' smiled Lestrade. 'This is not going to happen very often.'

No, I thought. *It has certainly not happened before.*

I concluded that he really was delighted to have pinned Homes down. Perhaps he genuinely had been pestering Sherlock to lecture although I had not been aware of the fact.

After the good and filling repast we all returned replete to the temporary lecture theatre.

'And now we reach the practical demonstration,' thundered Holmes, speaking much like a parson giving his weekly sermon imploring the congregation to join the throng of the saved. 'And this is where you can all take part.'

He looked round at the audience and picked on a young constable in the front row.

'You sir. What did you observe and deduce from the chair in question?'

The policeman nervously consulted his notes.

'It is a solid wooden chair with a padded seat covered in brown leather. There is damage to the leather seat in the nature of a small slit, perhaps made with a sharp object.'

'Good, good,' encouraged Sherlock Holmes. 'Did you make any other observations?'

'Only that the seat was standing four square facing a north-easterly direction.'

There was a ripple of laughter around the room at this latter comment. Holmes hushed the room and continued to address the constable who was now looking red-faced and embarrassed.

'Despite the laughter that was a good point. Now what do you see with regard to the position of the chair?'

The young constable hesitated and then stated that it was now facing north.

'Which is interesting,' expostulated Sherlock. 'As we can deduce the simple fact that during the tea break the chair has been moved slightly. Did anyone else notice that?'

The assembled company shook their heads and murmured in the negative.

'This young policeman has done very well, I think you'll agree?' queried out illustrious lecturer.

This was greeted with a splattering of applause.

'Does anybody have anything to add to the observations?' asked Holmes.

Another uniformed policeman put up his hand in the manner of an eager schoolboy and Holmes invited him to speak.

'The slit in the leather has a slightly rounded and turned-in appearance as if it was initially cut and then stretched,' stated the keen constable.

'Very good,' agreed Holmes. 'Any other comments?'

None were forthcoming so the great detective continued.

'You could have mentioned the label indicating that the chair came from the Heal's emporium on Tottenham Court Road. Or deduced the likelihood that the chair was one of a set of chairs. Or even that it is made in plain oak rather than the standard Queen Anne and Old English styles. You could have been more specific with regards to the cut which measures almost exactly two inches in length.'

Sherlock Holmes looked around the room and caught the eye of his elder brother.

'I forbad my brother Mycroft from commenting on the chair but I wonder if there is something he would like to say now about the appearances of the chair before and after the tea break?'

Mycroft cleared his throat and spoke in reply to Sherlock.

'Thank you brother. There are several observations I could make but I will limit my comments to just one. Before the excellent tea and cakes the chair was sporting but one damaged area on the leather seat. Now careful examination will show that there are two. The second is very difficult to see but definitely present.'

A hubbub of surprise greeted this utterance.

'Apart from myself had anybody else noted this fact?' asked Sherlock.

Nobody answered except for a few shaking heads so Holmes continued.

'So we have several facts. Firstly a damaged chair that I was fortunate enough to purchase from Heal and Sons. Secondly the design is one of the newer type designed by the young Ambrose Heal. Thirdly there was initially only one area of damage but now there are two. Add to that the fact that the chair has moved despite my instructions to observe but not to touch and we can conclude that somebody had a burning desire to handle the object.'

Holmes looked closely at the audience as he went on to his next lecturing point.

'As my brother Mycroft said there are many more observations and from them more deductions that could be made but I will stick to the relevant facts and provide a little more information about the chair. Ambrose Heal is in the audience today and he will be able to support my statements.'

Ambrose Heal stood and gave a little bow.

'The chair,' continued Holmes. 'Is indeed one of a set of six and Ambrose initially considered that the damage could have been caused by a disgruntled member of staff who did not like the new range of furniture. I was able to reassure him that this was not the case.'

As Holmes spoke I noted that four of Lestrade's men had stood up and moved to the windows and door such that nobody could leave without passing them.

'You may wonder how a consulting detective such as myself could have the time in my busy schedule to give a lecture to this small but august audience?'

I found myself nodding. I was indeed wondering such a thing.

'You might also wonder why I am not out searching for the Mayfair Ruby?'

Again I found myself nodding.

'I shall recount the details of the theft of the ruby,' stated the detective. 'The huge red stone set on a gold ring has recently been known as the Mayfair Ruby but was originally set into the head of an idol in a small temple outside Kathmandu in Nepal. More recently it was owned by the Richelieu family who had it set into the gold ring and just last week it was on display for sale in a most respectable jewellers in Bond Street. The price was one million pounds.'

There was a collective intake of breath at ·the mentioned figure. Sherlock Holmes looked round the room. Whereas his lecture on deduction and reasoning had resulted in some blank looks the audience were now captivated. There was nothing like a bit of larceny to catch the attention of the constabulary!

'The thief walked into the jewellers in broad daylight and then ran out having grabbed the ruby ring from the display cabinet. Two security men and a policeman on duty to guard the ring had their attention elsewhere at the time but soon set chase. The pursuit continued up Bond Street, across to Regent Street, thence to Oxford Street and finally Tottenham Court Road. At no time was the thief out of the sight of the pursuers but when he was finally apprehended in Heal and Sons furniture store he did not have the ruby ring. He could perhaps have thrown it away on route but such an action was not observed and the pursuers were adamant that they were only a short distance behind him at any moment. The man swore his innocence stating that he thought the people chasing him were wanting to rob him. He had not been seen actually handling the ring and his guilt had been assumed since he had been in the shop when the ruby went missing. Without the presence of the ring on his person and with only circumstantial evidence the police force would have to let him go very soon. So Lestrade called me in immediately.'

The inspector nodded to indicate that this was indeed the

truth. Sherlock's discourse continued.

'The very perspicacious staff at the furniture store had closed the doors of the room where the supposed thief was apprehended and only the two security men, the policeman and one shop assistant were near enough to have taken the ring off the man. He had no time to dispose of it in the shop so if he did have it where did it go? Fortunately a more senior policeman arrived on the scene very shortly after the man had been caught and he searched all five, the supposed thief and the policeman included. The ring was not found nor was it discovered in the store despite a fingertip search.'

There was a pause whilst the facts were mused upon by the audience.

'I was called later that same day,' continued Sherlock after the short breathing space. 'I visited the jewellery store and the furniture emporium and at the latter I noticed something amiss. A set of five dining chairs. I enquired about the sixth chair for dining chairs are sold in sets of four or six, sometimes even eight but not five.'

Ambrose Heal nodded vehemently at this point.

'I enquired about the sixth chair and discovered that it had minor damage which was going to be repaired. At that point I decided to purchase the set of all six, the damaged one included.'

Holmes smiled benignly at his audience.

'The chairs were delivered to my rooms at Baker Street and I carefully examined the damaged chair. I removed the leather from the seat revealing a disturbance in the padding. At the end of this grooving was the gold ring with the huge ruby set into it. I returned the ruby to the rightful owner and it is partly from the reward received that Inspector Lestrade has been able to provide the splendid tea and even more marvellous cakes.'

Lestrade beamed round at everybody.

'But the culprits …how could we ascertain whether the sequestration of the ring had been done by the thief or by an accomplice. And if it was the latter which of the four was guilty?'

Again Sherlock looked round the room.

'The first person to reach the supposed thief was the constable but how could he have hidden the ring so quickly? Were the security men involved? Was it the shop assistant, a respectable lady of thirty years experience?'

I looked round and imagined that one of the ladies in the audience could have been such a person whilst the other was clearly a lady policewoman.

'My examination of the highly polished ring revealed no fingerprints but there was something more to say about the chair. As described by an astute member of the audience the cut was slightly stretched as if an oval or round object might have passed through the small slit. Such an object could have had a diameter at the most of one and a quarter inches. This would have been much too small for a hand to have penetrated the seat stuffing.'

There was a slight movement at the front of the audience as if one of the policemen had decided to leave. He started to confer with Lestrade at the door to the room and I could hear him say that his period on duty started soon. Lestrade ordered him to sit down.

'But what could penetrate the stuffing, what object would be about that diameter and could have been used to push the large ring deep into the stuffing such that it was not found?

It took me a matter of moments to consider the Billy club. The truncheon that the police all carry if you are in uniform. Perhaps the policeman had pushed the ring deep into the stuffing!'

Once again there was some disturbance in the front row but Sherlock ignored it.

'But there was no proof so I suggested today's lecture and demonstration….and here we have our thief!'

The arguing policeman was stood up by two plainclothes men and his hands held high. They were bright red.

'Caught redhanded,' remarked Lestrade.

'I took the liberty of putting some dye into the stuffing of this particular chair,' remarked Holmes. 'And this is not the original seat. That is still in my rooms.'

'You'll regret this Holmes,' screamed the corrupt policeman. 'And you Lestrade. I've plenty of friends in the police force who would like to see you both come a cropper. You've crossed the line and bitten off more than you can chew, just you wait and see.'

The plainclothes detectives let out a whoop of delight as they found a large red ring in the policeman's pocket.

'And now we have found a ring in his pocket,' remarked the famous detective. 'A ring I had deposited in the seat padding, in order to capture the thief. But how did the policeman manage to hide the real ruby ring? He was passed the object by the original thief and quickly slit the adjacent chair and pushed the ring out of sight. It could not be found unless the chair upholstery was taken apart. But he did not reckon with the sharp eyes of Ambrose Heal, a man who was not present when the thief was apprehended. Ambrose noted the damage soon after the disturbance in the store and took the chair away for repair, unaware that the ruby ring was hidden in the seat squab. The policeman returned to ostensibly take statements from the shop assistant but in fact he was searching for the chair with the damage. The chair that I correctly deduced had been removed for mending.'

Sherlock Holmes stared at the policeman who was struggling with the detectives.

'How frantic our policeman must have been when he found no damage on any of the chairs. He probably searched all around the store as similar though not identical chairs are to be found in several of the rooms. Then Lestrade and I made sure that he knew about the lecture and the fact that seemingly unknowingly I had purchased the very same damaged chair from Heal's that he was looking for. We also arranged that the shop assistant and the two security men were here and that this place was secure.'

The policeman was still fighting the detectives but they were not perturbed. Big man though he was they had him firmly gripped and soon had handcuffs on him.

'The security men will be pleased to know that the policeman purposely distracted them in the jewellers in order that the thief could take the ruby ring,' stated Holmes. 'His distraction was insufficient as the absence of the ring was too quickly detected. It was then that our criminal law enforcement officer decided to join the chase and take the ring to hide it. The shop assistant is also here,' Holmes indicated the lady in the third row. 'And we have thus been able to completely exonerate her and the security men. This concludes my lecture and practical demonstration of my methods of detection and deduction.'

There was thunderous applause. Lestrade lead the handcuffed constable to the cells. As we left the room I heard

Mycroft remark to Sherlock.

'Well young brother you owe me ten guineas.'

'Why?' asked Sherlock, obviously piqued.

'The truncheon was eighteen inches long as I predicted, not the twenty that you deduced so I win our little wager.'

Sherlock laughed. 'I shall win next time. Just you wait and see.'

We walked back to number 221B Baker Street and on route I asked Sherlock why we had needed my presence and why he had enquired about the revolver.

'I hoped that my subterfuge by way of a lecture would work,' replied Holmes. 'But I was not sure. The most risky part was taking the chair from the lodgings to the police station. A typical criminal might have decided that he should attack at that time so you were invaluable as an escort. A policeman is not, however, a typical criminal. Not typical at all.'

'But why was Mycroft involved?' I enquired. 'It can't surely be about a wager. He wouldn't stir himself for that!'

'The ring was only worth stealing if there was a buyer in the offing,' replied the great detective. 'And there was…. a very senior man from a foreign embassy. Mycroft will be asking him to leave the country quietly.'

'And the ring that the policeman had in his pocket, the one he took from the demonstration chair…..'

'Was a cheap ring from a haberdashery store onto which I glued a red glass stone. The ruby thieves were well and truly conned.'

NOTE

The next tale was inspired by the stories of the First World War which are emerging now, one hundred years later. It is fiction but the situation was real....

Ghost Train

We moved along last night. In the cover of darkness we left our dugouts and as quietly as possible moved along the trenches to join up with the Canadian, Belgium and French soldiers already in position.

The Brits call the place we are defending Wipers but being a bilingual Canadian I know how to pronounce the name of the place. Ypres, pronounced ee-pray. But its real name is Hell.

The part we are in is definitely part of the Underworld. I can't tell you about the town itself but it must be pretty bad if this is anything to go by.

At times it feels that we are the only ones supporting the whole damn line, eh? Princess Patricia's Canadian Light Infantry. We've been in the line since April 9th and we've lost seventy-five of our men already, dead or injured. Our orders for tomorrow are to move back to a more defensible position whilst leaving enough men in place to give the impression that we are holding the front line. It could be worse. I could have been a private in the 1st Canadian Division like my pal Etienne. He was gassed along with hundreds of others when the Germans attacked at Gravenstafel Ridge. I've spoken to some of the French soldiers who were there. It sounds diabolical. A cloud of yellow gas swept over them as they waited in the trenches. The foul stuff was heavier than air and it rolled down into the shallow gullies, filling them and displacing the breathable air, burning the eyes, the nose, the mouth, the lungs. The men were coughing up blood and those that died went black almost immediately, bodies fell all around. Hell on Earth in what should have been the beautiful Spring month of April.

Some of the men leapt out of the trenches and were immediately shot down by a hail of gunfire from the Germans. Etienne never made it out of the dugout.

We are luckier, if you can count it as luck. Our medics have told us to put urine on towels and to breathe through the wetted cloth. Apparently the ammonia counteracts the chlorine and the gas is survivable that way.

But the attack left a bulge in our defenses and we are trying to plug it. If the Germans had moved forward quickly they could have broken through and taken Ypres but they were too afraid of their own damn gas. So, despite the fact that a huge section of the defensive line disappeared, the enemy did not take much advantage from it.

*

We have been heavily bombarded with mortars so the

battalion is moving back during the night to the better line of defense on the Ypres side of the woods. We are the last to go, taking occasional potshots at the enemy to give them the impression that the line is still intact.

By 3.00 a.m. the entire battalion had withdrawn to the new line with no discernible casualties. We were the last to join them and it was with some considerable relief that I slipped into the new trenches, the new line of defense.

The relief was short lived. The Hun were furious next morning when they discovered the ruse and immediately moved their heavy artillery into position to bombard our new line.

Relief by the Shropshire's came too late for many of our men. I am still OK and I have been told that I am to withdraw to the GHQ line with Lt-Col Buller.

*

Buller got it, struck in the eye with a shell fragment. I saw it happen and tried to get to him but another shell burst right near me with an enormous noise and I was knocked unconscious by the blast.

When I came round I was in a ditch. I could not hear a damn thing except a ringing in my ears however I carefully sat up and examined myself. I had a wound on my head that did not feel too bad and complete deafness, otherwise I was unscathed. But where was I?

I had not taken much notice of my surroundings being obliged to just follow wherever our commanders led and doing so with a crowd of other raw recruits and regulars. Not all of the men in the regiment were old originals. I had volunteered and joined the regiment just a few days before being sent to Ypres.

I looked round. It seemed to be dusk so I must have lain in the ditch all day, unnoticed. Or perhaps more than one day?

I stood up slowly in the gloom and found my way to a dusty road. I followed this for several miles but did not appear to be getting any closer to my destination. Where were all my compatriots? Where were the ruddy Germans for that matter?

As the light faded and darkness fell, I slipped and plunged down into an unseen culvert. I hit my head again but did not pass out. When I regained my footing I could see a silvery sheen stretching like a single lane road below and to either side of me. Then I decided that it was not a road but a railway, a hidden track for trains.

Silently, for my entire world was silent, a strange train drew up next to me. Only two carriages long, despite the darkness I could see a ghostly fire at the front and smoke billowing from an odd chimney.

Knowing that I was hopelessly lost and realising that the native Flemish were undoubtedly on our side I decided to climb aboard.

I opened the door that presented itself in front of me in the gloom and, clambering on to the eerie vehicle, I gratefully sat down on the nearest seat. With a shudder and a slight sway the train started off again. I looked down the carriage. It was entirely empty so after resting for a while I walked along to the end of the carriage and peered through into the next. I thought that I could see people in the next compartment but the carriage was not lit up and the darkness was very profound.

The train, moving exceedingly slowly, turned a long corner and came out of the culvert. There was a little more light and I could tell that none of the people in the other compartment were actually moving. I tried the communicating door but could not open it.

I now had to sit down again, I was feeling very light-headed and presumed that it could be due to concussion.

The train seem to be moving round in a very large curve and I was afraid that it might take me back in the direction I had come from, back towards the Germans and the inevitable bombardment. My somewhat addled mind summonsed words into a poem or song;

> *Ghost train, don't take me back*
> *Ghost train, don't take me back*
>
> *I'm relying on you, Ghost train*
> *Don't take me back to hell again*
> *Trusting you, Ghost train*
> *Don't take me back to hell*
>
> *Only way from this hell of mine*
> *Is to stay on this long dead line*
> *Ghost train stay on the track*
> *Ghost train don't take me back*
>
> *Ghost train, don't take me back*
> *Ghost train, don't take me back*
> *Ghost train, don't take me back*
> *Don't take me back to hell.*

I found myself singing the song mixed in with the words "We are holding up the whole damn line," the two weirdly merging at times into a delusional thought that somehow I was floating and holding up the train above me. At other moments I imagined that I had already died.

I tried looking out of the opposite end of the carriage but all I could see was mist, obscuring the line, obscuring the countryside, obscuring the world.

I vomited suddenly, bringing up only bile. Feeling nauseated I decided to lie down.

Then, as of nowhere, a conductor appeared in front of me.

'Avez-vous un billet?' he asked in deep, solemn tones. 'Do you have a ticket?'

'No, no,' I stammered in reply.

'Then you will have to get off the train at the next stop,' commanded the conductor.

As I looked more closely at him I could see that his face was that of a skull with burning red eyes. Where I had thought he was holding a ticket machine I observed that he was grasping a sickle.

'Yes, yes,' I replied once more, this time more quickly. 'I'll be happy to get off at the next stop.'

*

When I awoke I was in a hospital bed. My pal Roger was looking at me with a queer expression on his face.

'We lost you, mate,' he announced. 'Thought you were dead, eh?'

'How did I get here?' I asked, relieved that my hearing had returned.

'Floated here,' he replied.

'Floated?' I asked. 'On a ghost train?'

'Gee, I suppose it was a train of sorts,' replied Roger. 'But it looked more like a couple of barges or narrow boats to me.'

'Narrow boat?'

'Yeah,' answered Roger. 'You floated down on a boat on the

canal, right into the middle of Ypres. You were unconscious, of course, and we weren't sure if you were going to make it. But you have done. Well done mate.'

'So when do we go back to the front line?'

'You're not going back,' answered my pal. 'And neither am I.' He held up his left arm. The hand was missing.

'I reckon we've had a luck escape,' stated Roger, ruefully.

'A lucky escape from hell,' I replied.

My pal Roger nodded his head as he repeated what I had said.

'A lucky escape from hell.'

NOTE

The above story is entirely fictional but the setting, the canal, the gas, the bombardment, the enormity of the losses and the heroism of the Canadian soldiers are all true.

For more information about the Princess Patricia's Canadian Light Infantry

http://www.birthofaregiment.com/birth-of-a-regiment/background/background/frezenberg/

Now we move to the present. Although fictional the next story really could happen....

More Sherbet than Schubert

'Percy!'

Mary's voice rose and then fell in exasperation as she addressed her husband of forty-five years. Percy was going to a disreputable bar again to watch sport. This was a relatively new activity for her husband who had always been rather a timid, stay-at-home type. In fact, his only outside activities had been with the local church.

'It's no good repeating my name dear,' replied the stentorian tones from the object of her concern. 'I'm off to see the big match on the large TV at the Swan and Halfpence and I won't be back till gone midnight.'

Like a miniature Brian Blessed, Mary thought to herself. *He's always speaking in such deep, loud tones. It fair gives me a headache. I blame the choir for all this. Their success has given him far too much confidence.*

*

The choirmaster of the Lesser Ponting Male Voice Choir sat back in his chair reading through some choir music. Lesser Ponting was not a large place and he felt he had good reason to be satisfied with what he had achieved. When he had arrived at Saint Jude's, Lesser Ponting, some three years before, the choir had been moribund. There were no female members anymore and no boy choristers. There was just a ragbag of men who had been in the choir for more than twenty years and continued to arrive at choir practice every Friday night and then to "lead" the singing at the two services on a Sunday. "Lead" was really a euphemism since most of the time they fumbled their way through whilst the organist grimaced at their unfortunate efforts. In fact the vicar had decided to close the choir down just at the time when he, Peter Betterson, had arrived. Peter had persuaded the parson to give them just a few months more under his choral guidance and, after a very shaky start, they were now very popular.

The same old members were there and a few recruits had joined them. They had renamed the choir "Ponting's Harmonisers" .... or perhaps just simply named it since it had no formal appellation previously.

Initially the going had been tough. They were set in their ways and did not want to try new music. The basses had trouble reaching the lowest notes and the tenors could not reach the highest. As for the counter-tenors! Peter could not bear to think what they had sounded like. However, they were now taking outside engagements and had won several competitions. Peter was convinced he would soon have them performing on television. All it required to set them right was a few pieces of his partner's delicious friendship cake.

*

Betterson is a strange one, mused Bertie Swag, the organist. *Always giving them cake and insisting that they finish it.* He couldn't stand friendship cake himself and luckily Peter Betterson did not try and make him eat it...but the others were persuaded to consume the stuff in vast quantities. In fact Betterson's partner, Gloria, individualised the cake for each choir member. Some had walnuts in, others had pine nuts. Some had no nuts at all and several were made with soya milk and oil rather than with dairy products. Gloria seemed to be able to conjure up a recipe that suited each individual. *There are so many food allergies these days*, Bertie considered. *But Gloria seems to be able to find a way round every form of hypersensitivity.*

*

Eric Matthews and Cuthbert Grand were the two counter-tenors. Both had been married with children until the last eighteen months but they were now living together. These were the singers who had so worried Peter Betterson that he tried very hard not to remember what they had sounded like. Now they sang like angels whilst holding hands at the back of the choir and giggling like schoolgirls.

*

Peter Betterson was still looking through his extensive library of scores. The choir had mastered the Messiah. Perhaps they were ready for Schubert's part songs for male voice. Some people did not take Schubert's songs seriously. The harmonies were very sweet, bringing to mind barbershop quartets...more sherbet than Schubert . Peter was not worried about that. The quality of his choir was now so good that the Schubert would win over even the most cynical critic. The World was his oyster and the choir his pearl.

*

The choir practice did not go quite so well as expected. There was some sort of muddle with the cakes which made Peter much angrier than Bertie Swag had expected. Bertie looked on with wry amusement as Betterson tried to sort it out and then refused to let anybody have the cake. When his back was turned the cake had disappeared and despite Peter's protests it had all been eaten.

*

The same thing happened at the next choir practice and Peter Betterson was becoming distraught. What is more the voices were not quite as good as they should have been.

Swag, in the confusion over the cake, had managed to snaffle a piece. He was going to get it analysed by his brother-in-law. He had his suspicions.

*

'Now then, sir,' said the large policeman who was knocking on the front door of the semi-detached cottage belonging to Peter and Gloria. 'Am I right in saying that your name is Mister Betterson?'

'Certainly,' replied Peter Betterson somewhat warily. 'What seems to be the trouble?'

'May I come in?' replied the policeman, entering the house as he did so. 'We have reason to believe that you have been a naughty boy.'

'I don't know what you mean,' blustered Betterson in reply and then shouted to Gloria, who was in the kitchen making the cake. 'Gloria. There's a large policeman here who says that I have been a naughty boy.'

Gloria popped her head round the door and then scurried back to the large modern kitchen. The policeman strode past Peter and followed Gloria who was hurriedly trying to put some large jars of pills and capsules into a top cupboard. It was, however, clear that she had been grinding them up with a pestle and mortar and sprinkling them into the cakes.

'Peter Betterson and Gloria Underwood I am arresting you on suspicion of administering substances of a pharmacological nature to unsuspecting persons. In short, on suspicion of poisoning,' the policeman put up a large hand to silence their objections. 'Anything you say may be taken down and used in evidence against you. You have a right to remain silent and a right to be represented by a solicitor...but, madam, stop trying to put that large jar of pills into that bin behind you. It will not do any good.'

*

'It was really Edwin that gave me the great idea,' said Peter to his solicitor. He was sat in a police interview room with his head in his hands, with just the solicitor for company. 'The choir was so bad and Edwin's voice was the weakest. He had been a very proficient bass singer, so they all said, but now he was struggling to reach the low notes. Mind you, he was nearly a hundred years old.'

Peter paused and sighed.

'Go on,' interjected the solicitor. 'Tell me how Edwin gave you your "great idea" as you put it. I need to know all the details if I am to help you.'

'Well, he had carcinoma of the prostate and he was being treated with hormones. Chemical castration they call it. It fights the testosterone or something. Anyway, I was convinced it had affected his voice. Raised it.'

'So?'

'So if it had worked for him it could help our tenors and counter-tenors. I went round to his house and borrowed some of his pills on a pretext. He didn't mind. Said I could have as many as I liked.'

'And you gave them to the choir?'

'It wasn't as simple as that. I don't suppose they would have just taken them if I had offered them so I got Gloria to bake a cake and I put it into each individual portion. Gloria had nothing to do with it. She thought it was a form of spice.'

'Except the bottle that the policeman took out of her hand had the words Flutamide anti-androgen on it.'

'Hey, don't be so aggressive. I thought you were on Gloria's and my side.'

'I am, but I have to understand what is going on.'

'Anyway....it worked and their voices improved. Then I thought why not help the Basso profundo with a bit of testosterone. So that's what they got.'

'And they improved?'

'They became amazing. Particularly Percy, his deep tones are terrific..and we started to win competitions.'

'Where did you get the drugs? You can't have got them all from Edwin.'

'No. Only the doses for the first two weeks. After that I got them on the internet with no trouble at all.'

'We'll have no problem getting bail for the two of you but this could eventually lead to a jail sentence. You really are not allowed to administer medicines to people without their consent and this could be construed as poisoning.'

*

'Well Peter. You and Gloria are very lucky,' the solicitor took off his glasses and wiped them. They had steamed up in the hot fug of Peter's front room. 'None of the choir wanted to press charges except for the organist who had eaten none of the cake and therefore could not claim to have been poisoned. It seems that they are very happy with the effects the medicine has had on them and want to continue. They will have to persuade their GPs to prescribe them because obtaining the medicines over the internet is the one crime that you must definitely stop..'

'And what are the police saying?' asked Peter.

'They are letting you both off with a caution,' replied the legal expert. 'But they are holding onto your computer until they have cautioned you and they will be monitoring your internet use.'

After letting the solicitor out of the front door, Peter went straight to the kitchen. Gloria was in her apron again with a big smile on her face. She was mixing a large creamy friendship cake.

'Get the pills dear,' said said with a grin.

'Certainly, love' replied Peter and ran upstairs.

The loft ladder came down with well-oiled smoothness and Peter climbed up.

The attic was completely full of boxes of pills.

They come much cheaper if you buy in bulk, Peter chuckled to himself. *Got to make some Schubert sherbet for the lads. We'll be on the TV yet.*

NOTE

More Sherbet than Schubert was inspired by a choir that my father helped to organise but at no time did the choir master poison the members of the choir with illicit hormonal drugs so please do not believe the story to be the truth.

I did, however, see a programme on television just the other night and the trade in illicit drugs on the internet is quite frightening. As a retired doctor I have to put my medical hat on and advise people against buying drugs from websites. They do not necessarily contain the medicine that they purport to and they are often contaminated and can kill. Do not take the story as being something to aspire to!

The next tale is a true story!

Processed Cheese

M y maiden aunt had lived on a strange diet of processed cheese and Mars bars for many years. This she washed down with copious cups of weak tea.

One day, about ten years ago when she was ninety, she phoned me for advice.

'Hello dear,' she whispered down the line. 'I've got no energy at all. What should I do?'

'Fruit,' I answered. 'Fruit and vegetables. You can't expect to feel energetic if you eat just cheese and chocolate.'

I tried to explain about Vitamin C, complex sugars, variety in the diet and other such ideas but my aunt was only half listening. She had only caught the first word.

Fruit.

She phoned me again a few days later.

'You were quite right dear. Fruit was the answer. I've been eating some fruit and I feel a lot better.'

'What fruit have you eaten,' I enquired, curious to know.

'Strawberry jam!' was her triumphant reply.

NOTE

The story *"Processed Cheese"*, would be flash fiction if it were not a true one. It is a reminder that the old adage truth is stranger than fiction may actually (and strangely) be true. It is also a cautionary tale not to take every thing the papers report doctors as saying to heart. We medics do not yet know the secret of really long life and it probably resides on the genes rather than in what you eat or don't eat!

I've told this little tale to many people and they usually laugh and then say something along the lines of....

"I expect a diet like that shortened her life."

I have to reply that I have no idea since she has just celebrated her centenary and is still going strong.

So if watch your diet don't take too much notice of the doctors. A little of what you fancy does you good and just make sure that your portions are not too large.

After that story about food we move to an Agatha Christie take off. This is a light hearted spoof of the Hercule Poirot stories and the peculiar world which Christie described where you were never quite sure whether it was set in 1920, 1970 or, as in this case, the modern day.

The Mysterious Affair
at Manorbier

'Monsieur Heracles Pernod at your service!'

A little dapper man with a twirled moustache executed a stiff bow as he introduced himself.

'Ah,' replied the colonel, a large, red faced, bluff fellow. 'The Belgian, I presume.'

'Mais non, monsieur,' Pernod shook his head. 'That is the other one. I am from France.'

'Right,' the colonel look just a bit confused. 'But you are a detective?'

'Oui monsieur,' nodded Pernod. 'Though embarrassé to say, I am rather more successful than the Belgian.'

'In what way?' asked the colonel.

'The other, he uses just the little grey cells. I like to use the whole of my brain,' explained Pernod. 'And I am very happy with modern techniques. Forensic science is très important.'

'Humph. The Belgian has a considerable reputation,eh?' hee-hawed the colonel.

'C'est vrai,' agreed Pernod. 'And it is particularly true in his own eyes.'

'But he has solved many cases...'

'After the murderers have struck again. Often several times when the Belgian is on site.'

Pernod pointed this out whilst waving his right index finger in the air to make his point. 'However, that is enough about him. How can I help you?'

'Maybe I have written to you erroneously,' harrumphed the colonel. 'I think that I meant to write to the Belgian.'

'If I do not manage to help you then please do consult the Belgian popinjay,' stated Pernod. 'And I only expect to be paid for results.'

'Well....' the colonel knew a good deal when he saw one and had realised that he might get a considerable amount of work out for Pernod for nothing whereas the Belgian was notoriously expensive. The colonel did not like having to pay for outside consultancy but his boss, the chief constable, had insisted,

'That's settled then, n'est ce pas?' Pernod correctly interpreted the hesitation as being agreement. 'Now who, what, where and when are your problems?'

'As you know,' replied the colonel. 'I am the deputy chief constable for that part of Wales and my team are flummoxed by the case that has presented itself.'

'In the castle?'

'Yes, indeed,' agreed the colonel. 'In Manorbier Castle.'

'Describe the affair from the beginning, if you please,' the Frenchman inclined his head, presenting a listening ear to the colonel.

'It's a typical locked room case in which only the dead

person could have done the crime,‘ explained the deputy chief constable.

'So why is it not suicide?' asked Pernod.

'She had no real reason to kill herself,' explained the colonel. 'And the note was enigmatic.'

'Enigmatic?'

'A puzzle really,' answered the colonel. 'It said No apologies. Then on another few lines random place names. Bristol, Brest, Naples, Manorbier, Maida Vale. Things like that.'

Pernod looked surprised.

'Here,' suggested the colonel. 'I have a copy. Take a look.'

Heracles Pernod stared at the note.

No apologies

Bristol…Brest, Naples

Manorbier Maida Vale

Preston to Iron Acton

Chard, Burnt Oak and Ashburnham

Bath and Poole.

'That was the suicide note?' Pernod raised his eyebrows. 'A very strange affair indeed. No mention of death, dying or despair, mon ami?'

'None at all.'

'Then why do you think it is a suicide note?'

'It was found by the body. The smoking gun was in her hand and she had blown her brains out.'

'Or somebody else had blown her brains out and left us a conundrum. Who was she?'

'The mistress of the local vicar.'

'The local vicar!' Pernod was shocked. 'Are the Anglican

priest's allowed to have mistresses?'

'This was an unprecedented occurrence,' stated the colonel. 'The local vicar was the priest for four different churches. He had no wife but had a mistress in each of the parishes. Most unfortunate.'

'And when he was found out...'

'He was defrocked, of course,' replied the colonel with a slight smile. 'A regrettable phrase as one imagines that he may have already defrocked himself many times in each of the parishes.'

'And this mistress is thought to have killed herself because she could not stand the shame?'

'So they say,' replied the colonel. 'And the doors were definitely locked on the inside so presumably it is true.'

'But the suicide note. It is most peculiar,' stated the Frenchman. 'I think that you will have to give me all the details, all the names and I shall come to Manorbier to help you.'

'Is there any light you can put on this strange affair?' asked the deputy chief constable.

'To start with?' queried the French detective. 'Certainement. Using seulement my little grey cells the note is a joke.'

'A joke?'

'A series of jokes, mon ami,' murmured the Frenchman. 'How do you say un calembour?'

'A pun?' the colonel was confused.

'But yes, monsieur,' nodded Pernod. 'The note is a series of puns. As yet I do not know if it relates to the affair or is purely une coïncidence. I shall go to Manorbier to find out.'

'Oh I see,' nodded the colonel. 'Man of beer, Maid of ale.'

'Certainement,' agreed Pernod. 'Pressed on and iron act on.

Both ways of smoothing clothes, non?'

'But why Bristol to Brest and Naples?' queried the policeman.

'You 'ave your cockney rhyming slang: Bristol City, titty,' suggested Pernod, twiddling his moustache as he spoke. 'Then Brest is obvious and Naples is similar to nipples. It is a homonym and, in fact, a homophone.'

*

The train left London's Paddington Station early in the morning. There would be just one change at Swansea to catch the Tenby train and this suited Pernod. He would eat twice in the dining car, he decided. First he would have breakfast at eight am, his normal time, then he would partake of coffee at 10.15 with a large sticky bun, arriving at Swansea by 10.45. He would catch the connecting train for Tenby arriving just before one in the afternoon, in time for his lunch, which he would take in a small restaurant on the front. Monsieur Pernod's secretary, Miss Linda Lime, had booked the tickets and a place in the restaurant with a table looking out to sea. Pernod did not like to do anything without a good deal of planning beforehand. If he sometimes made his detection and conclusion look easy it was solely, he believed, because of the work put in beforehand.

The colonel would meet him at the restaurant at two o'clock by which time Monsieur Pernod believed that he would have finished his lunch and be ready for another cup of coffee.

All went according to plan. The train shot past Reading, Swindon, Bristol and Cardiff. Pernod was unaware of the passing scenery. It was irrelevant and therefore best ignored and so he spent the time going through the rest of the information that the colonel had given him about the strange affairs of the village priest. Monsieur Pernod also worked away on his smart phone, sending texts, receiving emails and searching the internet... something he knew the Belgian would never have done.

The train arrived on time in Swansea. In fact according to Pernod's pocket watch it was five minutes early. But he was pleased to note that the Tenby train was exactly on time and he was soon descending into the town.

The walk from the station was only short but Pernod's precisely metered pace meant that it took longer than it would have done for most people. Despite this, or perhaps due to it, he arrived at the restaurant exactly as the local church clock struck one.

The meal was pleasant but not memorable and it was with a sigh that Pernod finished his last mouthful of dessert. He did miss French cooking.

*

'What do you say to going straight to the castle right now?' asked the colonel as soon as he arrived.

'Without having a coffee and a chocolate bon bon?' Pernod was horrified at the idea. 'All in good time, colonel. You must sit and tell me more about the case.'

'Harrumph,' coughed the colonel. 'Oh well, yes OK.'

The policeman sat down and started to go over the case again.

'Miss Natalie Bullmore is the girl's name,' stated the colonel. 'Though I shouldn't have called her a girl. The poor thing was forty-two years of age. Young to die but clearly no spring chicken.'

'Ah, poulet de printemps,' muttered Pernod.

'Eh what?' queried the colonel.

'Spring chicken. Such a delicate delight,' murmured Pernod,

smacking his lips.

'Well yes, quite,' replied the deputy to the chief constable, looking at Pernod as if he was some kind of weird tropical fruit. 'Where was I?'

'The girl was forty-two,' replied Pernod.

'Yes, no longer in the flush of youth so when the priest was defrocked and all the other mistresses came to light I can understand her shock and perhaps her road to self harm.'

'Too much for a call for help, mon ami,' Pernod shook his head. 'Blowing your head off with a hand gun is more than just self harm....such a waste.'

'The gun itself was an exhibit in a locked case in the castle.'

'And the bullet came from the gun?'

'We imagine so but the bullet was a dum dum and had shattered into many pieces so forensic evidence is not that easy.'

'An exploding bullet!' exclaimed Pernod. 'The woman must have been in a terrible mess.'

'Most of her head was blown off,' agreed the colonel.

'But was a bullet shot from the gun?'

'Indeed and the remaining bullets were of the same type.'

'Hand guns are banned in Britain. Why was the gun kept at the castle?' asked Pernod.

'It was an exhibit, supposedly inactivated,' remarked the deputy chief constable.

'But not so....'

'Obviously not.'

'And the bullets?'

'Expanding bullets are in common usage for law enforcement.'

'Mais oui, it is the same in France,' sighed Pernod. 'Now I

have finished my coffee and we go the scene of the tragedy, n'est ce pas?'

*

The village of Manorbier was only about six miles from Tenby and the senior policeman drove quietly along the A4139 into the small township.

'Of course you could have taken the train all the way to Manorbier,' remarked the colonel.

'And miss my lunch?' Pernod was astonished at the suggestion. 'Non, non, non monsieur. That would never do. Ce n'est pas possible!'

'Almost there,' stated the colonel.

'Tell me more about the priest and the other mistresses,' suggested Pernod.

'Yes, quite right, remiss of me,' remarked the colonel. 'The Reverend Albert Samuel Asplen, though perhaps now I should call him just Albert Asplen.'

'And the others?'

'Three other ladies. Mary Slack, Evelyn Pearce and Joanna Jones.'

'And is it likely that they were involved?'

'None of the ladies has a convincing alibi,' replied the policeman. 'But the vicar was nowhere near the scene.'

'His alibi, you 'ave checked?' asked the French detective.

'He was definitely in London,' replied the colonel. 'His alibi has been corroborated by no less than two archbishops.'

'Two?'

'Yes, the Primate of all England was presiding at an appeal hearing accompanied by the Archbishop of Wales.'

'Probablement the appeal, it was for the Reverend Bertram Samuel?'

'Albert Asplen,' corrected the colonel. 'Yes. He was fighting against being defrocked on the grounds that Canon Law stated that no person who has been admitted to the order of bishop, priest, or deacon can ever be divested of the character of his order.'

'If that is so then he must have won his case, n'est ce pas?'

'No,' stated the colonel. 'They changed the law specifically to defrock him as an example. But his alibi is totally watertight.'

'Who discovered the body?'

'The gunshot and its echo were heard outside the castle. Two policemen were the first on the scene and they could not open the door since it was locked on the inside. They eventually forced the strong wooden door open and found a horrifying mess.'

'The gun was in her hand?'

'It was but her head was not really on her body.'

'Oh la la!'

*

They parked in a car park in Manorbier near to the strikingly preserved Norman castle. The hauntingly beautiful village nestling in a valley by the sea drew little response from the French detective. The sooner he could get back to his beloved city life the better. Everything should be in order and the countryside did not attract him one little bit.

As they walked from the car towards the castle Pernod did note that it was a rectangular enclosure with round and square towers. Whilst he was mentally considering these features the colonel was describing the life of the victim.

'She was the curator of the small museum in the castle and lived in the cottage in the grounds,' the policeman stated. 'Not much more to say about her. Very quiet. Her greatest delight, apart from the vicar, was doing the Times crossword each day.'

'And the priest? You told me something about him but I would like to hear more'

'Much more lively. Quite an interesting character. As I told you he was an army chaplain for quite a while,' the colonel looked a bit put out. 'Met him at a few army dos in fact. Adored by the troops, so I understand. They reckoned he was one of them.'

'And now?'

'He's rather let the side down, don't you know?'

'By having the affairs?'

'Yes, yes. Terrible business.'

'In France we do not make so much fuss about such things,' remarked Heracles Pernod. 'It is de rigueur for a prominent man to have affairs.'

'But not a priest, surely?' this time the colonel was shocked.

'No monsieur, but people such as you and I,' Pernod smiled. 'It would be expected of us.'

The colonel's already red face became almost beetroot with embarrassment.

'I hope you are not suggesting that I would do such a thing?' blustered the colonel.

'Non, non monsieur. Dieu ne plaise,' soothed Pernod. 'God forbid! We are in Wales not in France or even Belgium.'

Inside the castle the deputy chief constable led Pernod around the grounds. They stood on the broad green swathe of grass within the four strong stone walls and looked at the scene.

'That is the cottage that Miss Bullmore lived in, n'est ce pas?' asked the French detective.

'Yes,' agreed the colonel. 'It's rather beautiful don't you

think?'

'I would not like the, how you say, thatched roof,' replied Pernod. 'Too many insects, too much of the maintenance. Non, non. Not for Heracles Pernod.'

'But she didn't die in her cottage,' stated the bluff senior policeman. 'She was killed or killed herself in that part of the castle.'

The colonel pointed to a well preserved area of the wall. Two uniformed policemen were standing guarding the doorways and the entire section had been roped off.

'It is the museum,' explained the colonel.

'Can we go and see it?' asked Pernod. 'I would like to see avec mes propres yeux.'

'With your own eyes? Yes, of course,' agreed the ex-soldier who was now such a senior policeman. 'The fingerprint johnnies have already been in there so it should be no problem.'

As they walked towards the museum the colonel received a call on his cellphone.

'Right, I see, fine,' he finished the call and turned to the Frenchman. 'I may have wasted your time, Pernod, old boy. That was a call from the forensic boffins. They have put the bullet together and they are convinced that it had been fired from the gun.'

'And only one bullet had been fired?'

'Yes,' agreed the policeman. 'I'm pretty sure that I have told you that at least twice. The magazine was otherwise full. Just one bullet missing.'

'It is good to be certain,' said the consulting detective.

'The point is that it simply must have been suicide so we do not need to waste your time any more.'

'Ne vous inquiétez pas,' murmured the detective. 'Do not

worry. You will only pay by results and suicide is not a result in my book.'

'Oh, fine,' the colonel brightened considerably. He did not mind wasting the stuck-up Frenchman's time if the police force did not have to pay and now the case really was almost certainly suicide it looked as if they would have no invoice. The senior policeman shrugged his shoulders. If Pernod wanted to waste his time, on his own money, then it was no problem.

The room, made of solid stone blocks, was long and narrow with two solid doors, slits for windows with no access from the inside of the castle and tall unscalable walls on the outside.

'Both door were definitely locked from the inside?' enquired Pernod. 'You have the word of the policemen?'

'Definitely locked from the inside.'

'And the telephone, the handset of the landline. Where was that?'

'The phone? It was lying on the floor next to the body.'

Pernod looked at the chalk mark where the body had lain. Blood stains were obvious at the head end and the body had been stretched out with the gun in the woman's right hand.

He looked down the room. At the other end on a small table was a large pumpkin. Painted on the pumpkin Pernod could see a face with small round glasses and a full beard.

'Qu'est-ce que c'est?' enquired the French detective. 'What is that?'

'That?' the colonel glanced where Pernod was pointing. 'That is a little joke from our philandering priest I expect.'

'A joke?'

'The pumpkin face looks very much like the reverend,' explained the policeman. 'He is a bit of a sculptor and artist I believe.'

'Zut alors!' exclaimed Pernod. 'An artist on pumpkins. Whatever next?'

Pernod looked around at the crime scene, examined the door locks and the thin slit windows and then turned to the colonel.

'I 'ave seen what I need to see for now,' the Frenchman shrugged his shoulders. 'I cannot add anything as yet but I would like to just visit the church before we leave.'

The colonel led the Frenchman out of the castle down into the valley and up towards the medieval church which stood part way up the hill on the other side of the dip. The distinctive white tower had been clearly visible from the castle and as they got near to the church Pernod could see a large notice.

CHURCH OF ST JAMES
MANORBIER
PEMBROKESHIRE
THE ANGLICAN CHURCH IN WALES
VICAR: REVEREND BERT S. ASPLEN

The final line had been vandalised and the unknown graffiti "artist" had scrawled Rev Up your A** in white letters over the vicar's name. Pernod had to suppress a laugh but the colonel was incensed.

'Whatever is the world coming to?' he snorted. 'Criminal damage to church property in a beautiful place like this. It's unbearable and I blame the vicar. His activities have brought the church into disrepute!'

After his initial amusement Pernod had stood stock still as if struck by lightning.

'What a fool I have been,' he suddenly said, shaking off the torpor that had grabbed him. 'We must return to the castle.'

There is little time to waste.'

The colonel looked at Pernod in surprise.

'Whatever is the problem, old boy?' he asked.

'Hurry, hurry. Vite, vite!' cried the French detective as he hastened down the road.

The colonel soon caught him up and they quickly reentered the ancient castle.

'To the murder room,' cried Pernod.

'So you do think it's murder now?' queried the colonel.

'Of course,' replied Pernod. 'Why would I be here otherwise? It's always murder when I am called in even when they have killed themselves, as in this most strange affair.'

They reached the scene of the crime and Pernod clapped his hands very loudly, nodded his head and then ran over to the far wall near to the pumpkin. He searched around then brought a magnifying glass out of his pocket. Finally, after some considerable time, he found what he was looking for. Now, taking a pair of tweezers from another pocket, he prised the object out of a crack between the solid blocks of stone. He then put the find into a small plastic bottle and passed it to the colonel.

'Here is the bullet,' Pernod remarked.

'Which bullet?' queried the colonel. 'We've already got the bullet that was fired from the gun.'

'A bullet that had, at one time, been fired from the gun but not the bullet,' explained Pernod, enigmatically. 'This is the bullet.'

'How can that be the case?' asked the colonel.

'Therein lies a tale but first we must gather all the suspects to us.'

'Why?' asked the colonel. 'If you know who did it surely it

would be more sensible and less dangerous to tell me and I will arrest him or her.'

'Where would be the drama in that, mon ami?' asked Pernod with a twinkle in his eye.

*

   The police station in Tenby was a whitish grey, rendered terrace house on Warren Street...... a name which had immediately put Heracles Pernod into a feeling of great nostalgia for the Victoria Line in London even though he had only left the capital that morning. It was nearly six in the evening and the Frenchman was now sure that he would not be able to return to the Big Smoke until the next day! Quelle horreur!

   The ex-reverend, Albert Asplen, was the first to arrive at the police station.In the interview room Pernod was busy patting cushions on chairs, fussing like a mother hen. The defrocked vicar strode in confidently.

   'Hello there,' a jolly voice emanating from his bearded face. 'I received the message from the colonel and came over straight away. How can I help you?'

   'All in good time mon ami,' beamed Pernod, secretly amused by the similarity with the painting on the pumpkin. 'But first I must introduce myself. I am Heracles Pernod, the famous detective.'

   'The Belgian?'

   'Non monsieur,' Pernod's moustache sagged slightly. 'I am a Frenchman and my name is Pernod, like the drink.'

   'Ah yes,' smiled Asplen. 'The successor to absinthe. An anise-flavoured liquor.'

   'You are very knowledgable,' Pernod executed one of his little stiff bows. 'I am a descendant of Henri Pernod himself.'

Just as he did so there was a kerfuffle on the stairs and three ladies under the age of forty entered, arguing noisily with each other. They were followed by the colonel.

'Let me introduce Mary Slack, Evelyn Pearce and Joanna Jones,' announced the policeman.

Heracles Pernod went up close to the women and bowed to each in turn and pointed to the cushioned seats.

The women reluctantly sat on the proffered chairs and it was clear that there was considerable animosity in the room. The ladies looked at each other with unconcealed dislike and occasionally glanced at Asplen as if to appeal to him. The dismissed vicar tried studiously to avoid their gaze.

When they were all settled down Pernod started his oration.

'I am, as you know, the great French detective, Monsieur Heracles Pernod,' he delivered another even more theatrical bow and then continued. 'I was asked by the Dyfed Powys police to look into this terrible business of the death of Miss Bullmore.'

'But why?' asked one of the ladies. Pernod had just been told that her name was Joanna Jones.

'Well Miss Jones,' replied Pernod. 'The chief constable asked the colonel to engage my services so I came.'

'Did you find anything useful?' enquired Evelyn Pearce. 'I understand that she shot herself in a locked room.'

'Well mon petit chou, I did find something useful,' beamed Pernod. 'I found out that they were right. The room was indeed locked from the inside.'

'Could anybody else have been in the room or somehow shot her from outside?' asked the third lady, Mary Slack.

'No my dear,' Pernod waved his finger. 'The room was impregnable and Miss Bullmore let off the last shot from the handgun.'

'So it was suicide!' exclaimed Albert Asplen. 'How tragic!'

'My feelings indeed,' agreed Pernod. 'Exactement that which I initially said. Est-ce pas, colonel?'

'Yes, yes,' harrumphed the colonel, looking somewhat embarrassed. 'It's what we all thought. Except perhaps the Chief Constable.'

'Who is a friend of the parents of poor Miss Bullmore, ai-je raison?'

'Yes you are correct. He is indeed,' answered the senior policeman. 'Or so I believe.'

'And then we thought the case was proven when we received the information that the pieces of bullet found within the shattered head of the poor Miss Bullmore were indeed shot from the gun in question.'

'We did, we did,' agreed the colonel somewhat reluctantly.

'Then why are we all here?' asked Asplen. 'I, for one, have work to do.'

'What work would that be, my friend?' asked Pernod.

'You are, in an underhand way, referring to the fact that I have been dismissed from my position of vicar of the four parishes,' sneered Asplen, his initial charm and goodwill having disappeared. 'And that is true but I am still a writer of some repute and many magazines are interested in my story. I am also an artist with an exhibition in the offing for which I must prepare.'

'Which, I believe, will include some of your own jewellery, designed and made by your own hand?' Pernod asked this with his head tilted slightly to one side, his right eye staring at the ex-priest.

'Is that a crime?' asked Asplen. 'Because if it isn't you can get off my back.'

'And you made the unique pieces that the ladies in the room are wearing?'

Pernod pointed at each lady in turn as he said this and it was clear that the chunky ornaments they were sporting were rather similar in nature. Two had very heavy necklaces and the other had a large brooch. They were clearly made of gold but included precious stones in abstract design.

'That is true,' agreed Asplen. 'But why are you asking me these strange questions?'

'Perhaps just to point out that you treated all of the ladies the same and gave them your own unique creations?' Pernod twinkled his reply.

'That is true,' nodded the ex-parson.

'C'est bien!' exclaimed the French detective. 'But now I must get on to something more serious. The alibi!'

'Wait a minute,' exclaimed Evelyn Pearce. 'Why do we need alibis if poor Miss Bullmore killed herself?'

'Mais oui,' replied Pernod. 'I have not explained myself well. Suicide was not an option in this case.'

'Why not?' asked Miss Pearce, bristling with irritation.

'Because I, Heracles Pernod, say so, mademoiselle.'

'So how do you account for the fact that she shot herself in a locked room?' asked Albert Asplen.

'Do not rush me,' replied the infuriating Frenchman.

The colonel sighed...was this going anywhere useful? He doubted it.

'So first the alibis,' the French detective with the ridiculous moustache looked round the room and picked on Evelyn Pearce. 'You, Miss Pearce, your alibi is that you were out for a walk by the seaside. You say that you met no-one at the time in question. Even though you started in Tenby and returned much later you could have reached Manorbier on foot.'

'Don't be daft, you silly man,' replied Pearce. 'It's far too far!'

'Less than six miles and your whereabouts is unaccounted for all afternoon.'

Pearce shifted uneasily in her seat.

'Mary Slack,' Pernod pointed at the red head. 'You claim to have been asleep in your room all afternoon. Again no witnesses. Did you go to Manorbier?'

The woman shook her head in denial.

'And Mademoiselle Joanna Jones,' the beautiful woman shifted uneasily as Pernod moved the attention on to her. 'You claim to have been in the church in Tenby arranging flowers. For some reason once again there were no witnesses.'

'That's not at all unusual,' replied the shapely brunette. 'The church does not receive many visitors on a Friday.'

'So three people who might have a grudge against Miss Bullmore but do not have an alibi,' Pernod turned and faced the ex-priest. 'And you, perhaps the most likely to wish her harm, yet your alibi is perfect.'

The bearded defrocked parson nodded with a slightly sardonic smile on his face.

'Or is it?' asked Heracles Pernod.

'Of course it is!' exclaimed Albert Asplen. 'I was with the Archbishops of Canterbury and of Wales. What better alibi could anyone have? And why do you imply that I may have wanted to harm poor Natalie?'

'Now let us consider the conundrum,' remarked Pernod in reply. 'The lady in question is in a locked room, the gun is in her hand, only one bullet is missing from the gun. There is no way of shooting her from outside and there is a note in her own hand which is peculiarly enigmatic.'

Pernod distributed five copies to the ladies and two gentlemen.

No apologies

Bristol... Brest, Naples

Manorbier Maida Vale

Preston to Iron Acton

Chard, Burnt Oak and Ashburnham

Bath and Poole.

'No apologies could be a reference to her suicide,' suggested Asplen. 'The rest are just random place names.'

'I don't think so, my friend,' replied Pernod. 'I used my little grey cells and came up with the suggestion that they were puns..... perhaps twinning of cities humoristique. For example we 'ave Man of Beer twinned with Maid of Ale. A male person of an alcoholic yeast-fermented malt drink flavoured with hops and an unmarried female also of the same drink.'

The long explanation left most of the people in the room looking puzzled then they realised what Pernod was talking about and could not help but smile slightly.

'So they are all puns,' remarked Asplen. 'To write puns when she was about to kill herself shows that she could not be in her right state of mind.'

'It is very unusual, indeed, my friend but who commits suicide in a normal state of mind?' asked Pernod.

'Exactly!' declared Asplen. 'So can we go now?'

'Not so quickly,' countered Pernod. 'I will contend that the writing shows she was indeed in a normal state of mind and that she was killed unlawfully.'

'This is rot!' cried Asplen, jumping to his feet. 'And I, for one, will listen to no more of it.'

'Sit down, Bert Asplen!' commanded Pernod in a firm voice and the ex-priest reluctantly concurred. 'Now I shall follow the logic further. Who can get into a locked room with all entrances sealed?'

'Nobody!' exclaimed Joanna Jones.

'Precisement!' agreed Pernod. 'But people can be influenced from outside a locked room.'

'Now we're talking poltergeists, spiritualism and such balderdash!' cried the ex-priest, jumping to his feet again.

'Sit down please,' harrumphed the colonel. 'This won't take much longer.'

Secretly the colonel was thinking that he would break up the meeting soon if Pernod did not get to the conclusion of the gathering.

'No monsieur,' replied the greatest French detective. 'We are talking about radio, we are talking about telephones, mobile phones, TV, the internet, email. Even written letters. It is fairly easy to influence someone by these means even though they are in a closed, locked room.'

'But it would still be suicide even if someone persuaded them to do it,' muttered Evelyn Pearce.

'Not if the influence was more direct than simply psychology,' replied Pernod. 'And that is what happened.'

'Nonsense!' shouted Asplen. 'This is a concatenation of balderdash. I won't listen to any more.'

The man jumped to his feet and strode to the door, turned the handle and found the portal was locked.

'I took the precaution of locking the door,' remarked Pernod, holding up the key.

'I didn't see you do that!' exclaimed the colonel.

'Prestidigitation,' replied Pernod. 'But I continue. Persuasion was part of it and this was over the telephone wasn't it Bert Asplen?'

'Why do you ask me?' demanded the ex-priest, leaning against the wall near the locked door. 'I have no idea.'

'Yes you do,' retorted Pernod. 'When you spoke to Mrs. Asplen on the telephone you riled her so much that she pulled the trigger of the gun!'

At the words Mrs. Asplen there was an audible intake of breath by all three women and by the colonel. Only Albert Asplen was unmoved.

'Who do you mean? asked the ex-priest in imperious tones.

'Your wife, who was known by all as Miss Natalie Bullmore, a name she kept for professional purposes, but who you had secretly wed ten years ago when you were in the army.'

'Is this true?' asked the colonel, looking from Albert Asplen to Pernod and back again.

'C'est vrai!' replied Pernod. 'I have been checking each of the women and the Albert Asplen when I was on the train this morning.... and I believe that the recently revealed dalliances of the reverend led her to ask for a divorce.'

'It's all nonsense,' exclaimed the ex-vicar. 'Everybody would know if I was married. A vicar's wife is an important institution in a small place like this.'

'Would they know if the wife wished to keep it secret because she was an avowed humanist, like Natalie Bullmore?' asked Pernod. 'But anyway it is a matter of record that they were married.'

'OK,' Asplen lifted his hands up. 'I admit we were married. It alters nothing.'

'But you could not afford a divorce, could you my friend?' asked Pernod. 'You have a small income from a trust fund but most of your salary is from the church. You will now get a pension but you did not want to share this with your wife, nor did you wish to share your trust fund.'

'She was on a salary from the castle,' replied Asplen.

'Untrue,' replied the Frenchman. 'That I also checked. She was an unpaid voluntary worker, much respected but unpaid, nevertheless.'

'This is all rubbish,' blustered Asplen. 'How could I have killed her from a distance?'

'You were on the telephone to her and goaded her so much that she pointed the gun at the pumpkin and pulled the trigger.'

'The pumpkin? What are you talking about?' screamed Asplen.

'I am talking about the painted pumpkin that looked so much like yourself. The goad to anger which you had so carefully and so purposely placed in the museum.'

'Rot!'

'Non monsieur. It is not rot. The pumpkin, it is in place at the far end of the room. You know that your lady wife has the habit of playing with the gun and clicking on the trigger and pointing at targets when alone in the locked museum. To her this is perfectly safe as she knows the gun has been deactivated. On the day of her death she is sat at her desk...as always at exactly the same time each day. You telephone and you purposely get her annoyed. The gun, that she thinks is deactivated, she picks up and as you talk she pulls the trigger, pointing the gun at the pumpkin. There is a huge bang and, as it happens, she misses the target.'

'That is a stupid idea,' shouted Asplen. 'Shooting at a pumpkin would not have blown her head off. She must have done it purposely! She must have known what she was doing and committed suicide.'

'Non monsieur,' Pernod shook his head wearily from side to side. 'Because that was not the bullet that killed her!'

'So what killed her?' sneered the ex-priest.

'The bullet that killed her had been carefully fired and then the pieces collected some time before,' explained Pernod. 'It was then placed with a small but highly lethal and destructive charge in the chunky halter necklace that poor Mrs. Asplen wore round her neck. You, Reverend Asplen, on hearing the bang that you knew meant she had fired the gun, pressed a small device up against the telephone receiver. This, by clever electronic means that I do not pretend to understand, ignited the explosive around her neck, blowing off part of her head and leaving the fragments of bullet embedded in the remainder.'

'You don't know what you are talking about,' the former priest looked round the room at the three women and the colonel who were staring at him in amazement. 'He admits that it is all beyond him. It is obvious that I could not do something like that. It would require enormous skill and knowledge of electronics. You must all see that it is a tissue of lies and I could not possibly have made something so complicated.'

His voice was mellifluous and convincing.

'Err, yes. It is a problem,' agreed the colonel. 'Monsieur Pernod, how do you reply to that?'

'My dear colonel,' responded the Frenchman. 'You should know the answer to that yourself. Albert Asplen was in the army!'

'Of course I know that,' snorted the colonel. 'But he was only a chaplain. He didn't work with electronics or bombs. They don't let chaplains loose on things like that. It would be far too dangerous.'

'True, true,' agreed Pernod, his eyes twinkling and his moustache vibrating with glee. 'But you told me that the old boys from the army loved him and thought he was one of their own. So I checked on his army career. Albert Asplen was not always a chaplain. Before he took holy orders he was in the bomb disposal unit and was one of their most capable officers.'

Asplen was busily searching in his pockets, his demeanour was becoming more and more disturbed as he failed to discover the object he was looking for.

'Is this what you want?' asked Heracles Pernod, holding up a small electronic device.

'Give it to me!' screamed the ex-priest.

'I don't think so,' retorted Pernod. 'And ladies, I should remove the chunky jewellry that Asplen gave you. It might be bad for your 'ealth.'

The priest lunged wildly across the room trying to get at Pernod but the colonel stepped forward, a service revolver in his hand.

'Sit down and stay still Asplen,' ordered the colonel. 'Or I will shoot you and I am still a crack shot. The game is up.'

*

The ladies had left. Asplen had been cautioned and taken into custody and Pernod was sitting once more in the small restaurant, studying the menu. The colonel was sat opposite him and obviously wanted to understand the reasoning behind Pernod's astonishing success.

'What was it at the church that made you change your mind?' asked the colonel after Pernod had ordered his meal.

'Mais oui,' explained Pernod. 'It was such a simple thing and I realise I had been such a fool.'

'What was it?'

'The man's name on the board. Bert S. Asplen. It is obviously an anagram of the two words Brest and Naples.'

'But why did that make you change your mind?'

'I realised that this expert on crosswords was doodling when she wrote the words. The anagram amused her so she wrote it down. Perhaps she had thought about it before like a friend of mine whose name is Lois.'

'Lois? I don't understand.'

'Her anagrams are soil, silo, oils.'

'Yes, OK,' the colonel was perplexed. 'Why did that spark off the other ideas?'

'Mademoiselle Natalie was clearly speaking on the phone as she was doodling. It is the sort of thing that people do. Asplen was not apologising and was annoying her. She noted Bristol down....perhaps because she had decided to arrange the divorce through some lawyers she knew in that city. She was a very private person who would not have liked local lawyers to know what she was up to.'

'And Maida Vale?'

'That is where Asplen was phoning from and the similarity with Manorbier would have amused a crossword expert.'

'Preston and Iron Acton?'

'Asplen had worked in Preston and Natalie was interested in a chapel in Iron Acton. But perhaps it was simply because of the pun that she doodled the words.'

'Chard, Burnt Oak and Ashburnham?' queried the colonel.

'And Bath and Poole?'

'They are obvious puns. Charred wood and burnt oak, mon ami,' Pernod looked at the colonel with surprise. The English usually understood wordplay better than the French.

'I see the jokes,' explained the colonel, just a little perplexed. 'But why was she writing it at all?'

'You have to realise that she had absolutely no idea, aucune idée, that her demise was near,' replied Pernod. 'She was doodling as she talked.'

'So basically the note meant nothing?'

'That's right but, mon dieu, it made me realise that the phone was a crucial part of the story.'

'But how did you know about the bullet in the wall?' asked the colonel. 'That was a stroke of genius.'

'I realised that there must have been two shots, or at least a shot and a small but lethal explosion and I decided that the most likely target for the first would have been the ghastly pumpkin head.'

'But how did you know that there were two shots?'

'The witnesses described an echo but when I clapped my hands hard in the room I noticed no clear echo. So I looked for the bullet and found it.'

'But how did Asplen make the gun work when it was supposed to be deactivated?' asked the colonel.

'Mon cher monsieur,' replied the infuriating Frenchman. 'It was all worked out by Asplen over a period of time since 'is affairs were made public.'

'So he stole the gun and played around with it?'

'The man stole the gun and replaced it with one he had in his own collection. Many ex-soldiers have illegal guns and he reasoned that his wife would not notice the difference. He was so right, so murderously right.'

'Was it just because of the divorce that he killed her?'

'Je ne pense pas. I don't think so,' replied Pernod, waving an index finger. 'But watching him with the women I believe, monsieur, that he wished to continue his affair with one of them. Perhaps the beautiful Miss Jones. His chances would have diminished considerablement if 'e was in the throes of a messy divorce.'

'So you will be sending us a bill, Mister Pernod,' stated the colonel. 'And this must rate as one of your greatest successes.'

'Non monsieur, I will not be sending you a bill,' the colonel looked surprised as Pernod continued. 'But my secretary Miss Linda Lime will do so, certainement.'

The colonel stood up and the waiter appeared with Pernod's order.

'Thank you,' said the colonel. 'You've saved the reputation of the police force.'

'And maybe the lives of the other three ladies,' nodded Pernod. 'Il est vrai!'

The French detective smiled as he pulled out his pocket watch.

'But now I must eat. It is exactly huit heures, my suppertime!'

NOTE

That was the first of two stories in this anthology of the locked room, smoking gun genre. You will come across the other later in the book but next I take you briefly into the world of aberrant pets. Many people keep rabbits in a pen. This one was kept in a cage......

Rabbit Love

As narrated to Paul Goddard by Stephen Goddard

(author of "Rattles and Rosettes")

Martin was chagrined. He had not loved his rabbit enough and that was the cause of its bad behaviour. This much had been made clear to him by his friend Neil.

Martin had thought that the problem lay within the rabbit. When he had first bought the male, long-haired Angora rabbit the creature had been very lovable. They had dutifully combed and groomed the pet on a daily basis. The rabbit had the run of the ground floor of the house and was allowed out into the garden. It had popped back into its cage with no trouble at all and was loved by the whole family.

Things had taken a turn for the worse recently. The rabbit was now very large and had become aggressive. In fact, Martin could no longer allow it out around the house or garden as the young children were really scared of it, as was next door's dog! The rabbit stayed locked up in its fairly large cage.

To feed the animal Martin had to close one part of the cage, put in the food and then remove the partition. If he tried to just put the food directly in, with the rabbit loose, he risked being bitten by large rabbit incisors.

Now Neil had explained it all to Martin. Apparently what had happened was that Martin and the family had withdrawn their affection and this had disturbed the animal. For the rabbit to be rehabilitated all that was needed was love and tender care.

Neil was a hippy. Maybe now a retired hippy but still a hippy. Flower power and love were his passion, animal welfare his hobby.

Watched by Martin, Neil had taken the rabbit out of the cage and placed it gently on his lap. Martin had not dared to handle the animal for weeks but now Neil had spoken words in a loving tone to the animal and it had calmly allowed itself to be picked out and stroked.

'There, there you beautiful thing,' breathed Neil. 'Did your family forget you. Neil won't desert you. Neil loves you.'

Then Neil started singing, in a rather weak voice, an old lullaby from Ireland.

'Toola roola roola' he crooned, his voice becoming more melodic as he continued. The rabbit lay quietly on Neil's lap as the retired hippy stroked his long, somewhat matted, hair.

'Golden slumbers kiss you eyes....'

Before anymore of the song could be sung the rabbit leapt up and sank its teeth into Neil's scrawny neck. Neil leapt up in alarm trying to shake the beast off but the long-eared and long-haired monster clung on.

'Get it off me, help! Help!' cried Neil becoming progressively more panicked. Blood was seeping down from his neck and staining his favourite paisley shirt. 'Help!'

Martin tried to pull the rabbit's jaws apart to no avail. Despairingly he grabbed a cricket bat and lightly hit the rabbit. Again, the rabbit clung on.

'Hit it harder,' gasped Neil, all thought of love and compassion having disappeared. 'Thump the bastard.'

Martin complied, taking a good swing and dislodging the brute. The rabbit lay stunned in a corner as Martin hastily compressed a towel against Neil's bleeding neck. By sheer good chance the Angoran rabbit had missed the main blood vessels. Martin sat Neil on a chair and contemplated whether he should get him to lie down. However Neil waved his hand to dismiss further attention.

'Just get your psychopathic killer before he wakes up or he'll be chasing us round the kitchen,' he said to Martin.

Martin looked over to the rabbit and sure enough it was already stirring. He ran over and grabbed the pet and locked it into its cage.

'So much for free love,' remarked Neil. 'I always thought it was overrated.'

*

Enough is enough, thought Martin as he walked down to the pet shop with the rabbit in a box. *I will take this creature back to the shop that I bought it from.*

The pet shop owner was pleased to see Martin.

'I'll buy him back off you,' he agreed, having heard the entire story. 'Can't give you quite as much as you paid since he is a good bit older. But we can use him to breed more rabbits. He's a pedigree Angoran so he will be a jolly good stud.'

NOTE

Thank you to Wikipedia and Loggie-Log for the rabbit picture which I have adapted.

Worryingly enough that was, in essence, a true story. As is the next one. All names have been changed to protect the innocent...

Whisky

Sean Macfarlane furrowed his Neanderthal brow. This waiting around was beginning to vex him. He was an important person, didn't the hospital know that?

For the twentieth time he stood up and looked around, flexed his biceps and exercised his shoulders. Usually that got people running but the medical staff just ignored him and carried on with their work.

He shouldn't have hit the man so hard with his bare fist.

I should have thumped him with a hammer, thought Macfarlane. *Then I wouldn't have broken my bloody fist.*

He looked at his hand, swollen and painful. He'd been in Casualty at the city's Royal Hospital for four hours. Back and forwards he had gone to X-ray, the casualty officer had taken a look at him and now he was being sent back again for another view.

He'd told the doctor that he'd thumped a door but the man had clearly not believed him.

Sean's day had not started well. He'd gone down to the benefits office and the woman in charge had clearly not believed him when he said that he'd not been working and had no money.

'I'll have to give you the benefit of the doubt,' she'd told him with a cynical grin. 'But I'd prefer to give you the doubt of the benefits.'

What was the cow talking about? Sean was not able to understand any subtle humour.

Now he was going in to see the casualty officer and the doctor was prodding his painful fist. His meta-crap-all, or something like that, was fractured. Or so the doctor had informed him.

'So it's not broken then, doc?' he had asked as politely as he could muster.

'Of course it is,' the doctor had replied in an obvious tone of condescension...an attitude that Sean could detect but not a word that Sean would have used or readily understood. 'Fractured and broken are the same thing.'

'Does it need any treatment?' he had asked the so-superior doctor, when in fact he would have preferred to hit him on the nose.

'I'll need to manipulate the bones and reduce the fracture, then we will have to put you in a plaster.'

'Well hurry up about it, can't you?' demanded Macfarlane.

'Yes, OK,' agreed the doctor. 'I was thinking that you might need a GA but if you can stand a bit of pain I could do it under local.'

'Is GA when you put someone out?' asked Sean

'That's right,' smiled the doctor with a truly irritating grin. 'GA means General Anaesthetic but we can't do that immediately because you've been eating and drinking recently. We would have to wait until tomorrow morning.'

'I don't want no-one putting me out,' Sean had replied.

So now he was waiting while they got things ready in the Casualty small ops theatre to do the reduction under local. They were going to take another thirty minutes before they were ready for him so he stood up and prowled off down the corridor.

The doc was wrong. He hadn't been eating. He'd been drinking. He was supposed to be going out with the gang for a curry later but at lunchtime he'd had a skinful. He'd punched the bugger at twelve noon. The man in the pub did not know who he was talking to and had refused to give up his stool when Macfarlane had wanted it.

Sean was the leader of the library. The library is what Sean called it as he thought it sounded cleverer than gang or club. He called it that because they kept a book on who could get away with the most criminal acts in a week. Presently Macfarlane was well in the lead and if that was still the case at Christmas he would win the jackpot which presently stood at just over one thousand quid. So it was a library with just one book which one member had said was ironic. Sean liked to be ironic as it sounded tough like a man of steel. Yes, he liked ironic. He did not know what it meant but he liked the sound of the word.

And Sean was certainly tough. Six feet and four inches tall, built like a tank. But he had punched the man on his jaw and broken his own fist. His meta-crap-all.

I should have used a hammer.

The fact that he had not had a hammer handy did not worry Sean. If he had used a hammer he would not have broken his bloody meta-crap-all so it was obvious that he should have used a hammer.

Sean loped along the corridor creating a patch of scowling darkness around him as he went.

'Buy a raffle ticket. Just one pound for a strip,' came a querulous voice.

Sean looked round at the unlikely sound. Nobody interrupted Macfarlane when he was in a bad mood.

A little old lady was standing in front of a stall of bric-a-brac.

A pile of rubbish is what Sean thought.

'Buy a raffle ticket, come on young man,' said the wrinkled old lady.

'What's it for?' asked Sean.

'It's in aid of the scanner appeal,' replied the old lady eagerly. 'I've already raised nearly one hundred thousand pounds from this stall but we need a lot more.'

'No,' Sean was angry at being misunderstood. 'What is the main prize?'

'A big bottle of Glenfiddich whisky,' replied the sweet old dear, holding up the item in her left hand. 'One of the best single malts. It's a special distillery edition.'

'Don't drink whisky,' replied Sean with a sneer. 'I drink beer.'

He exhaled noisily over the poor soul.

'I can smell it,' she answered, reeling back. 'But you could still have a ticket. If you win you could give the bottle to a friend. It would make a great gift....and there are plenty of other prizes.'

Sean picked the bottle from the brave lady's hand and took a look at the amber liquid.

'Yeah,' he finally stated. 'But I don't have friends. I just have people who do what I say.'

He roughly placed the bottle down on the surface and walked away.

'Thanks a bunch,' shouted the lady after the retreating back. 'Thanks for nothing.'

*

Back in Casualty, or the Accident and Emergency Department as they insisted on calling it, the medical staff were ready for Macfarlane. They took him into the small operating theatre and laid him down on a hard operating table.

'The local will be quite uncomfortable,' the casualty officer informed him. 'LA does sting quite a bit.'

'Just get on with it can't you?' insisted Macfarlane. 'I've got a dinner date tonight.'

In reality it was a very fluid arrangement. A few more beers then off for that curry with the lads from the library. Macfarlane grinned at the thought. Almost killing a random dude with one blow to the jaw counted as an offence to go in the book so he was further ahead of the others in the library gang. He had a second laugh when he thought of the fact that none of the guys ever went to a library. As far as he knew he was the only one who could read and he could only do that if he used his finger for each word and read out loud.

'Owww! What the frack was that?' Macfarlane had stopped grinning.

The local anaesthetic was worse than a bit uncomfortable. It was stinging like fury.

'That frackingwell hurts!' exclaimed the bully and gang-leader.

'The sting will wear off pretty quickly and your hand will go numb,' explained the doctor.

After a few minutes the doctor tried waggling Sean's hand. Previously any movement had been very painful but now there was just a residual dull ache.

'OK,' smiled the casualty doctor. 'I'll see if I can reduce the fracture.'

He pulled sharply on Macfarlane's hand and pushed downwards at the same time. Despite the local anaesthetic Sean winced with the pain but the job was done.

'Not too difficult,' pronounced the doctor. 'That should do it. Are you OK?'

He projected the question to Sean Macfarlane. The big man looked up from the table.

'I'm OK,' he answered. 'But no thanks to you. You should have done that earlier.'

'Yes, well that's one form of gratitude for our hard work,' replied the doctor. 'Now I have to immobilise this. We'll use some self-gripping rubberised bandage.'

'Do it good and proper, doc,' ordered Macfarlane. 'I don't want it getting out of place and I want something to show for my time. I want a proper plaster.'

'Right, OK,' agreed the casualty officer, nodding his head. 'But first we must take another X-ray to check its position. So no jostling with it. Go straight round to X-ray then back here for the result.'

Sean hated being told what to do by anyone and it would have been no use explaining to him that it was all for his own benefit. The same argument had been put to him throughout his schooling and his reply had come as a straight quote from the mouth of his father.

"They get paid for it, don't they?"

*

X-ray was not very busy and when he came out Sean saw that the little old lady with the raffle was nowhere to be seen. The woeful prizes were standing in a row but pride of place was reserved for the big bottle of malt whisky. Sean hesitated for less than a second before picking the bottle off the stall and placing it inside the bundle of overcoat and sweater that he was carrying. He walked on without breaking his stride, challenged by no-one.

Back in Casualty the team were waiting. The doctor, a nurse and a medical student were stood by a different couch which they beckoned Sean towards.

'OK,' said the doctor. 'The X-ray looked fine so we will plaster you up as you wish but you will have to return on Sunday morning to the hand clinic.'

'I can't come on Sunday and you haven't had time to see the X-ray yet,' protested Macfarlane.

'The X-ray is digital these days,' smiled the doctor in an avuncular manner. 'So it arrived here before you did. You can see it on the screen over there.'

The casualty officer pointed towards a smart flat screen on which Macfarlane could see the bones of his hand.

'Looks like a skeleton's hand,' he muttered.

'That is the general idea,' answered the doctor.

He really is gearing up for a punch on his nose, thought Macfarlane as he lay down and the medics started on the plastering.

'First we put a roll of bandage in his palm,' the doctor explained to the medical student.

Now he's ignoring me and teaching a fracking student.

'Then we curl the fingers over the roll. If you just plaster the hand without the roll it becomes very uncomfortable.'

Still talking to the student and ignoring me! Macfarlane let out a little growl.

'Did that hurt? I'm very sorry,' said the doctor, not sounding in the least bit contrite. 'Now we'll put on some netting, then the plaster.'

'Do you usually use a plaster bandage?' asked the student.

'No, not these days,' replied the casualty officer.

Macfarlane shifted a little in irritation that he was being talked over.

'Please try to keep still,' said the doctor. Macfarlane growled again.

'Nearly finished,' remarked the annoying medic. 'Now here are your plaster instructions and here your head injury instructions.'

'OK,' replied Macfarlane. 'But when do I come back if I can't come on Sunday?'

'I'll book you into the hand clinic for Monday morning,' the doctor informed him. 'Can you make that?'

'I expect so,' grunted the cave man as he got up off the couch. 'If I have to.'

'The plaster will have to come off or you fingers will seize up,' replied the doctor.

*

When the huge man had sloped out of the department the medical student, who had been watching the surly fellow disappear, turned back to the doctor.

'Thank you for letting me help,' she said politely.

'No trouble,' replied the casualty officer.

'Just one thing,' continued the student. 'I can understand why you gave him the plaster instructions but why did you give him the head injury instructions?'

'You saw how we plastered his fingers with the index and middle stuck out in a Churchillian salute?'

'Yes, of course,' she replied. 'But the head injury instructions? He hasn't got a head injury.'

'If he goes round waving a V sign in everybody's face he soon will have,' replied the casualty officer with a throwaway laugh.

*

Sean was picked up from the hospital by one of Mister Wild's cars, driven by one of his chauffeurs. Macfarlane could ask for the occasional favour as he was one of Wild's most successful pushers. The benefits officer had been right in suspecting that Macfarlane was not short of money but it was not the sort of job that one could declare and, in any case, why should he do without his benefits? It was his right.

So the library gang were a group of drug abusers and pushers led by Macfarlane. Today's innocent faces are tomorrow's clientele could have been his watchword if Sean had ever heard of Tom Lehrer. He hadn't and the method of giving out free samples until people were addicted had crept into Sean's weak mind without need of any prompting. He now had a big following of addicts metaphorically lining his pocket with silver and the pockets of Mister Wild with gold.

But it was sensible to keep the big man on his side and so, when he was dropped off at his council house he gave the bottle of whisky to the driver with strict instructions that it was for Mister Wild himself as a token of Sean's respect. The driver had touched his cap in acknowledgement and Macfarlane felt even more important and bigger than his already huge frame.

*

The driver was back outside Sean's house an hour or so later just as he was going out to meet the other members of the library.

'Yeah?' he sneered at the man as he beckoned to him. 'What d'you want?'

'Mister Wild would like to have a quiet word with you.'

Why would Mister Wild want to see him? Perhaps to thank him for the gift, thought Sean as he readily climbed into the car.

Wild did not look as friendly as Macfarlane had expected. He was flanked by two guys almost as large as Macfarlane and definitely as nasty.

'So that was a token of your respect?' asked Wild.

'Yeah,' smiled Sean. 'You deserve it.'

Wild nodded and from behind Macfarlane a third large man appeared and hit Macfarlane on the head. Then one of the flanking bodyguards kicked Macfarlane in the gonads. He doubled over in excruciating agony. They then picked him up and dumped him back in the car.

'Drive him up country and kick him out somewhere cold,' said Mister Wild with an ominous wink to one of the goons.

*

The casualty officer walked down the hospital corridor with a slight swagger. He was happy in his job and proud of the work he did and it showed in the way that he strode along. He stopped in his track when he saw Mavis Giles by her stand.

'You look upset!' he remarked, running over to her.

'Someone's stolen the main prize for the raffle,' she answered sadly. 'Who would do that to a little old lady like me?'

'What was it?' asked the doctor.

'A very nice bottle of Glenfiddich whisky,' she replied morosely. 'A big bottle, special edition.'

'I think I saw that in the possession of one of my patients,' stated the casualty doctor.

'Was he a great big surly man with a broken hand?' asked Mavis.

'That's the one,' agreed the doctor.

'Well he was sniffing around here,' replied Mavis. 'I thought that he was a bit of no good.'

'Here,' suggested the casualty officer who was really quite a kindly man. 'Let me pay for another bottle.'

He searched around in his pocket for his wallet.

'No, no, no,' replied the little old lady. 'There's no need for that.'

'Then what will you use for the main prize?' asked the casualty medic, his eyes sweeping the stall and recognising the unsuitability for taking that role of any of the rest of the items.

'He didn't get the real bottle,' chuckled the old lady. 'I'm not so daft as to put that out where anybody could steal it.'

'So what was in the bottle that he took, Mrs. Giles?' asked the doctor.

'He'll have a right surprise when he drinks it,' laughed Mavis, a big smile lighting up her wrinkled old face and her sadness forgotten.

'So what was it?'

'Cold tea,' she answered. 'I filled up an identical but empty bottle with cold tea.'

NOTE

From an almost true story to a completely fictional one.

His Own Petard is set in the present day and the characters are exaggerated but true to type.

His Own Petard

Doctor Anthony (call me Tony) Grabson looked appreciatively at the full-length mirror.

Though I say so myself, he thought immodestly, *I really am a handsome hunk.*

Life was good for Tony. He was the Chief Executive of a large teaching hospital on a salary of over a quarter of a million a year with his annual bonus.

In fact, if all things go to plan my salary this year may top the three hundred and fifty thousand mark and I would then be getting more than Jan Filochowski, at West Hertfordshire Hospitals Trust, the highest paid Chief Executive in any of the hospitals.

Tony adjusted his tie and patted his stomach. Flat as a board despite the carbohydrates and alcohol.

Tony had a little secret which nobody in the hospital was told about. He was a Type 1 diabetic and if he over-ate he just took a bit more insulin ... none of that "watching calories" like some diabetics. If his weight went up, he just reduced his dose of insulin and allowed his diabetes to go slightly out of control. That soon burnt up the calories and he was back to his normal slim self. His private consultant in Harley Street was always telling him that he was being foolish but Tony was certain that he knew best about his own body.

Today he was at exactly his target weight and he injected a slightly larger than normal dose of Insulin as he knew he was going out for a big lunch. A gourmet Christmas lunch with a drug rep. Tony was very strict about relationships with drug reps. He had enacted a blanket ban on any of the hospital staff meeting representatives from drug companies for any form of hospitality. That way they all had to come to him and he got the first pickings. Trips abroad, consultancy fees......all of these came his way.

The annual bonus, thought Tony, *that really is something to look forward to*. Recently the emphasis had changed. Previously the clinical side was ignored and hospitals were rated solely on non-clinical criteria. These were mainly economic and they were still important but a fuss had been made about hospitals maltreating and even killing people. So now there were significant clinical targets as well. Tony felt happy to get involved in the clinical work especially when it meant cutting clinics and saving money. Fewer clinics and fewer in-hospital stays meant less chance of complaints from patients and it saved money. Two birds with one stone.

Reducing outpatients was one of Tony's targets. Take the diabetology department for example. Tony considered it to be superfluous. General Practitioners could treat diabetes so why have a department in the hospital? The same went for hypertension and a variety of other conditions. Let them be treated out in the community.... treating them at hospital just made them dependent. Perfectly good treatment for the masses, Tony considered and they could go further yet. For example .... getting more people on to "End of Life Plans."

That was a wheeze that Tony loved. In fact he would like to cut out Resuscitation completely. It was expensive and rarely worked. The cost in medical time and drugs was exorbitant for the tiny return and the successful cases only led on to further treatment and later death, so why bother?

Tony was medically qualified so he felt he had a right to get involved with clinical problems. He had registered but only worked as a doctor for the one year. After that he had joined the Department of Health and moved up through the ranks of civil servants organising the financing of new hospitals via Private Finance Initiatives (PFI). With the Coalition Government's accession to power the game had changed and Tony had decided to move out before he was pushed. The Chief Executive post had come vacant and a few nudges here and there had secured the position.

The great thing about this hospital was that it had not saddled itself with a PFI which helped Tony enormously. He could stay within budget with very little effort and his contract was very rewarding if he actually cut the overall expenditure. Very rewarding indeed!

Today he was going to the hospital late in the morning after "working from home," a euphemism for getting up late. Firstly he would be taking a flying visit to the Accident and Emergency Department before visiting the Intensive Care Unit and then on to his large free lunch. He was at loggerheads with Newton, the consultant in charge of Intensive Care. Doctor Gloria Newton was, in Tony's eyes, an old-fashioned anaesthetist who believed that the patients came first not the budget, or the targets. She refused to acknowledge that Tony had any right to interfere clinically. She was very proud of her success rate from resuscitation .... around twenty-five percent which was considerably greater than the average. She would not listen to Tony's views on the uselessness of resuscitation and continued to attempt it on all patients whom she considered may be helped. What is more Newton was over sixty, overweight and had a hairy chin so Tony detested her.

Tony's rise had not all been due to hard work and good fortune. He was not adverse to a little skulduggery if he thought it would advance his cause. Tony had a little trick that he had put in place that might stop Newton's success. He had gone round swapping vials on the emergency tray. The trays were laid out with big printed labels and the drug vial attached below. The vials themselves had the name on them etched into the glass but Tony had noticed that in the hurry of an emergency it was the printed label that the doctors and nurses read. Sometimes they checked the actual glass vial but often they just assumed that it was correct.

Tony often went round late at night dressed as a porter. He had keys to all of the wards and departments and rarely met staff as he had cut the numbers of night nurses drastically. On his rounds, unobserved, he had swapped many of the Atropine vials and put Pancuronium Bromide in their place. This was a synthetic muscle relaxant and it caused generalised paralysis of voluntary muscle. The patient would go limp and all breathing would cease so any hope of resuscitation would be gone unless the staff detected the subterfuge. If they did notice, the person who would be admonished would be the nurse for setting the tray up incorrectly.

This, Tony was sure, would save money by cutting out further unnecessary treatment on people who were near death's door anyway. In some ways he was acting as an angel of mercy.

In Accident and Emergency Tony expected to be met immediately by the casualty consultants but he was made to wait due to several clinical emergencies arriving simultaneously with a squeal of ambulance sirens. He looked impatiently at his watch and noted that it was rapidly approaching lunchtime. Making a decision he left the A and E department and walked to the lifts that would take him to the Intensive Care Unit. The elevator was crowded and very hot and Tony loosened his usually immaculate tie. As he stepped out of the lift he realised that he needed glucose. He had taken a larger than normal dose of insulin and he had not yet had the larger calorie intake that was commensurate.

As he walked into the Intensive Care Unit he felt his legs wobble, he sweated copiously and fell to the ground. A pretty nurse ran over to him and he grasped her hand.

'Sugar,' he cried but since he had called her honey the last time he had tried to get off with her she thought it was just a term of endearment. A trainee registrar came running over and cried out.

'The Chief Executive has fainted.'

The registrar lay Dr. Grabson on the ground, checked his pulse and breathing and lifted his legs in the air. Tony did not come round. Knowing that the treatment for fainting included Atropine the registrar asked to be passed a vial from the emergency tray. He injected the unconscious Grabson and within seconds Tony stopped breathing.The registrar shouted for further assistance and Dr. Newton appeared from her office. She immediately assessed the situation and noted that Tony Grabson had a slightly raised pulse, was very sweaty, was not breathing and was completely motionless. The registrar agreed that the pulse had always been raised which was unusual for a vasovagal faint.

They quickly moved Grabson into a bed and within a very few moments Newton, who was an excellent doctor, had intubated him and started ventilation. His unconsciousness was still deepening and the consultant appeared puzzled. His symptoms and signs were those of hypoglycaemic coma but surely they would have known if their Chief Executive was diabetic? He was renowned for having made the diabetologists redundant and sacking all the staff of the diabetic clinic. She looked at his abdomen and noted the tell-tale signs of multiple injection sites.

'Would you believe it, he is a diabetic!' she exclaimed loudly in surprise 'It wasn't a faint it was hypoglycaemia. Take some blood for glucose levels and give him a big shot of glucose intravenously.'

The intravenous injection worked immediately and Tony woke up to horror. He was lying in an intensive care bed with a large tube down his throat and into his trachea. He was breathing by courtesy of a ventilator and the ugly old Newton woman was leaning over him staring into his eyes. He could hear, see, smell, taste, and think but he could not move a muscle.

'I do believe he has woken up,' remarked Newton, observing the faint movements of the pupils. 'So why was he in respiratory arrest and why can't he move a muscle? What was in the injection you gave?' The last question was directed to the Trainee Registrar.

'It was Atropine,' replied the worried younger doctor. 'It should have helped a vasovagal faint.'

'But does nothing good for a hypoglycaemic coma,' added Newton. 'However, it shouldn't have caused paralysis. Perhaps he has had a stroke, a CVA.' She pondered for a moment. 'Or maybe there was something wrong with the Atropine. Bring me the vial.'

The nurse was dispatched to go through the sharps box which had been almost empty. No Atropine vial was found but the empty vial of Pancuronium Bromide was discovered.

'That's it,' cried the registrar and then added in a puzzled voice. 'Except it's not Atropine.'

'No, it's a muscle relaxant. You should have checked the vial before injecting the drug, whatever the nurse tells you,' Dr. Newton looked worried.'Bring me a few more emergency trays, please.'

The Atropine had been swapped on several of the trays and Dr. Newton told the staff not to touch the trays or the bottles.

'This is a police case,' she explained. 'This is deliberate tampering and could easily cause death. It may already have done so. We must get these examined properly for fingerprints etcetera and find out who had access to the stores of this drug. This is a very serious problem and if we catch the perpetrator they are going to prison for a long time.'

Dr. Tony Grabson heard all of this and wanted to run as far away as possible but he could not move an inch. He had been so sure that his exploits would not be attributed to him that he had not bothered to put on gloves. His fingerprints were on every vial. He contemplated this and considered that his future prospects were also vile.

*

Dr. Gloria Newton sat, smiling, in her office. Everything had gone according to plan. In front of her were eleven bottles of Pancuronium Bromide..... they were the vials that Grabson had swapped on the wards other than her own and Gloria would be giving them to the police. Dr. Newton was aware of Grabson's strange night rounds dressed as a porter and she had resolved to follow him. She had been fortunate enough to observe him swapping a couple of bottles around and, after he had left, she had gone round all of the wards checking the emergency trays and putting them right. She had collected the vials of the muscle relaxant, wearing gloves as she did so. The only trays left with Pancuronium on them were the five in her own ward and she was keeping a close eye on them. She knew that the drugs would be traceable to whichever pharmacy Grabson had obtained them from. The badges which doubled as electronic keys provided a central record of all the locked places and all the people who visited them so there would be a trail of Grabson's activity. So Dr Newton carefully set up Grabson for his fall.

Gloria Newton detested Grabson even more than he hated her. Despite having made a public display of surprise at discovering that he was a diabetic she was already party to the information. Grabson was not the only person in the hospital with a secret and, unknown to most, Gloria's partner was the consultant diabetologist who had been ignominiously sacked by the detestable Grabson. Her partner had known the Harley Street specialist who treated the Chief Executive and that specialist had broken confidentiality and spoken about Tony Grabson's behaviour because of his concerns. Gloria Newton knew about Grabson's habit of eating large meals at the expense of drug companies. She had purposely arranged for him to visit the Intensive Care Unit where she had intended delaying him until he became hypoglycaemic. The delay in A and E had meant that Gloria did not need to artificially detain Grabson and the insulin had inexorably had its effect.

Her trainee registrar was part of the trap since Newton knew that he had a worrying habit of not checking the bottles. Gloria had even planted the idea of giving Atropine for a bad vasovagal faint in the registrar's mind during conversation the day before. Sure to form the trainee had injected Grabson without checking the bottle. So Dr. Gloria Newton was then available to save the day and the Chief Executive was lying in one of her beds on a ventilator. Dr. Newton hoped that this would be a salutary lesson for her registrar and that the police enquiry would see the end of Doctor Anthony (call me Tony) Grabson as Chief Executive.

There were partial antidotes to Pancuronium Bromide but the drug only had a short action .... about three hours maximum.

Not really long enough for a potential murderer to suffer thought Dr. Newton, picking up one of the vials on her desk.

NOTE

Lavish trips laid on by drugs firms to 'sway' NHS staff? Health service officials earning thousands organising and attending extravagant events where companies promote their products?

If the above sounds fictional you should look at a recent report in the Daily Telegraph (http://www.telegraph.co.uk/news/nhs/11755884/Lavish-trips-laid-on-by-drugs-firms-to-sway-NHS-staff.html).

Perhaps the managers would not resort to swapping drugs around and maybe the doctors would not allow a manager to suffer.....or perhaps they would? With some NHS chief executives awarding themselves pay rises of twenty-five percent per annum whilst denying any rise to the actual healthcare workers anything could happen.

Acknowledgements to Wikipedia for the open source picture of a syringe.

The next story is set in Spain. It's fictional but the demolition of houses owned by ex-pats is certainly happening

Poetic Justice

'Three hundred thousand illegal buildings in Andalucia,' Brian stated to Barbara. 'And it's ours they decide to knock down.'

'It's not just ours that they're going to bulldoze, love,' replied his child bride, to whom he had been married for forty years. 'They're also knocking down the Simmonds' place.'

'Yes, that's true,' grunted Brian. 'But just up the road is a huge complex owned by the mayor who issued the illegal forms and made a packet from it. They're not knocking that down.'

'But he did go to jail,' muttered Barbara, wiping a tear from her eyes.

Brian was right. It was so unfair. They had bought the property in good faith. It had been done through a supposedly good realtor, witnessed by an official notary. All the documents had been put through the official channels and duly signed before they had paid a penny.

It was only after the event, when they had sold up everything they owned in England and moved into their little dream house with its tiny swimming pool, that the corruption of the officials had come to light. The people who were suffering now were all the little folk who had purchased the properties with absolutely no idea that the local government were in cahoots with the property developers and the houses should never have been built.

'And the mayor was out again after two months,' sighed Brian. 'Living in his huge mansion just up the road.'

'Which is also on non-urban land,' Barbara nodded her head. 'You're right love but we'll just have to grin and bear it.'

'We'll be left with nothing,' he groaned. 'We'll have to move back to England and hope we can be housed by the council.'

'Not many council houses these days, dear,' sighed Barbara. 'But we'll still have our pensions.'

'Which don't go far these days,' Brian pointed out. 'If we've got to pay rent there'll be next to nothing left. If only these SOHA people could get on and stop the bulldozing.'

'They'll probably succeed eventually, dear,' replied Barbara. 'But too late for us.'

Barbara reflected on the SOHA movement. Save Our Homes Andalusia was a group that were seeking representation in all the local town halls. It looked as if they might succeed but in the meantime the program of demolition was going ahead and nobody was receiving compensation.

If only they were fairer and targeted the corrupt politicians first it would not feel so bad, thought Barbara. *And how could it be within human rights to knock down the only home of a person who had purchased a property in good faith?*

Barbara lay awake all night thinking about the problem. The notice of demolition had been served on them with a piece of paper pinned against their front door. She knew that the ex-mayor would be lying in a plush double bed, sleeping peacefully. She had spoken to a maid who worked for the disgraced mayor and heard that the man was completely unrepentant. The maid spoke excellent English and had been teaching Brian and Barbara some elementary Spanish...after all it had been their intention to make this their home for the remainder of their days.

A thought came unbidden to her mind but she pushed it away for the night and eventually went back to sleep.

Next day was to be their last in the dream house as the demolition was scheduled for the following day, the notice they had been given was very short. The morning came and they packed all their belongings into suitcases and moved a little way down the road into a small hotel. Their money would soon run out if they stayed for any length of time so they would be booking a flight back to England as soon as possible.

Late in the night in the little hotel Barbara got up out of bed and told her husband that she needed to take some air. He grunted a reply and it was not until nearly time to arise that she returned to the small hotel and showered quietly.

Over breakfast they could hear the bulldozers moving in.

Their house was the only one due for demolition that day so the sounds of banging and crashing that Brian could hear could only have been from his dream house being destroyed. Every now and then he could hear angry shouting in Spanish, shouting which, despite their few lessons, he was unable to translate. Perhaps some of the SOHA group had responded to their plight and were remonstrating with the drivers of the bulldozers? The voices sounded Spanish but he had heard that in the past few months dozens of Spanish people had joined the struggle, having also been affected.

Brian had expected the demolition to take at most an hour or two but he could not bring himself to watch. He finished his breakfast and sat sadly with his wife drinking an endless supply of tea.

At lunchtime the noise had still not abated and peculiar whispers were coming back into the hotel. Eventually he suggested to Barbara that they should go and see what was happening.

Up the road they could see an almighty row taking place. The demolition experts had taken the right fork in the road whilst their own dream house was down the left fork and they could see that it was completely intact. The bulldozers had stopped but the ex-mayor's housing complex lay in ruins.

'What are they saying?' asked Brian, speaking to a member of the hotel staff.

'The mayor has taken out an immediate injunction to stop any further demolition near here,' stated the receptionist. 'He is saying that his house has been demolished incorrectly and that it is your house they should have torn down. The demolition team have replied that the paperwork is in perfect order, the complex is definitely illegal and that as soon as the injunction is lifted the demolition will continue.'

'But why have they hit the ex-mayor's house?' asked Brian. 'It was ours they said they were going to knock down.'

'It is poetic justice,' replied the receptionist, shrugging his shoulders. 'Leave it at that.'

And perhaps, thought Barbara. *Just perhaps, justice was helped by somebody turning that temporary signpost in the night and pinning the demolition notice to the mayor's house. Now I wonder who could possibly have done that?*

NOTE

The actions of the government in Andalusia have certainly worried many home owners on the Costa del Sol. Are you safe in your own home if the paperwork turns out, through no fault of your own, to be fraudulent? It seems not and some British owners of villas have had their houses knocked down.

Perhaps when buying a property in Spain you need an attribute that the protagonist in the next story possesses?

Second Sight

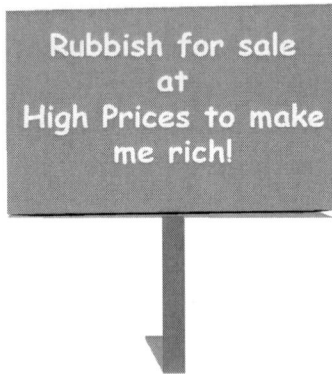

'Ok doc, here's the story. It started when I was looking through the classified section of the local paper in order to buy something,' the worried looking man was sitting in the doctor's examination room talking to his general practitioner.

'I see, Mr Jenkins,' replied the doctor nodding his head wisely. 'What happened?'

Jenkins heard this in his right ear but simultaneously could hear the doctor's thoughts in his left ear. *He's a bit out of date looking in the paper. I would have thought that he was bright enough to search Gumtree or Preloved on the internet. Or to bid on ebay.*

The confusion of information from left and right slowed the patient down but he finally replied.

'I have found that you can get good bargains through the local paper as the sellers are not quite as clued up as those using Gumtree or ebay,' he stated to the GP, talking a little primly. 'And because it is local you can inspect the goods before you buy.'

'Yes, yes, quite,' answered the GP but simultaneously thought, *Good point, I must have a peep in the local rag next time I want to buy something.*

'Thank you,' the patient inclined his head and raised a finger. 'But the point I was going to make was that the advertisements were all wrong.'

'How do you mean wrong?' asked the GP and his attention was now focussed entirely on Jenkins, his thoughts matching his words.

'I was looking for a guitar amplifier and instead of saying something like "**Good condition Marshall amp for sale**" I read the advert as **Clapped out old amplifier but it's all I've got left and I'm skint so I hope somebody is fool enough to buy it.**'

'Did somebody really put an advertisement into the paper that was so blunt?' asked the family doctor. His thoughts were perplexed.

'No they didn't,' replied Jenkins. 'That's the point really. When I screwed my eyes up and squinted at the paper I could read a completely normal advertisement. **Much loved Marshall guitar amplifier, only £95.**'

'And that's why you have come to see me?' asked the GP. *Not much to go on,* was what Jenkins could tell he was thinking.

'No, no,' Jenkins shook his head vigorously. 'It didn't stop there. I looked at the front page and read **We hate motorists. Get on your bikes you lazy bums!**'

'Surely that wasn't right?' queried the GP, leaning forward with a smile on his face.

'No. When I squinted it read: **Council introduces twenty mile per hour speed limit**. Quite different.'

'Did you read any more of the article?' asked the doctor.

'I did and it was very difficult. On first reading I was getting: **We know it will cause more pollution because the vehicles will be going round in lower gears for longer but we have to do something to justify our Green Capital status and we really do hate cars.**'

'And on second reading, when you squinted?'

'It was quite the opposite. It stated: **The limit is being imposed to improve the air quality.**'

'Yes, very difficult and very different indeed,' the GP nodded sagely but thought. *What the heck is going on here?*

'Then I looked at the personal adverts to see if they had changed,' said the patient.

'Had they?' asked the doctor.

'Definitely,' grimaced the patient. 'I glanced at the **Hookers seeking clients section.**'

'Is there one?' asked the GP in surprise.

'Sorry, with squinted vision it read **Ladies seeking Men**,' replied Jenkins. 'In that section I read an advertisement with my eyes narrowed and it read **Beautiful Oriental Lady needs male friend.**'

'And what did it say when you had your eyes wide open?' the GP was very interested now.

'It read: **Pox-ridden whore from the East End of London**

seeking rich marks.'

'What happened next?' asked the GP as he simultaneously thought *Is it Tourette's syndrome?*

'I had a feeling that this had all happened to me before but I had forgotten,' recounted the patient. 'Then I felt very anxious and sweaty and just sat there for some time.'

'Did anybody see this happening?' asked the family doctor whilst thinking...*Ah hah! I'm beginning to get an idea what this is all about.*

'Yes,' affirmed Mr. Jenkins. 'Mrs. Jenkins was watching me and she says that after reading the paper and squinting I then sat wide-eyed and motionless. Then, after some minutes, I sort of woke up and felt confused.'

'Right,' intoned the GP. 'I think I have the answer.' *Ruddy heck, he's got Temporal Lobe Epilepsy but the new sort I've just been reading about.*

'OK,' the patient prompted the GP to continue.

'I believe I may know what is wrong with you. Did you have any episodes of what we would call "aura" previous to the occasions you are describing or have you had any since then?'

'My wife tells me that I have had several similar episodes before but I must point out that this was the first one I could remember.'

'And since then?'

'Several times and on each occasion it was as if I could read the inner motives of the writer or hear the hidden thoughts of the person talking to me.'

'And now?' *Can he read my thoughts?*

'And right now I'm hearing your thoughts as well as your speech,' replied the patient.

Bananas and custard thought the doctor.

'Bananas and custard,' said the patient.

'Amazing!' exclaimed the doctor. *Bloody hell!* he thought to himself.

'You were thinking bloody hell,' stated Mr. Jenkins.

'Sorry about that,' replied the GP. 'I will have to try to keep my thoughts on the straight and narrow. But you need further investigation.'

'What will that require?' asked Mr. Jenkins.

'MRI and CT,' replied the GP. 'What you have is Temporal Lobe Epilepsy with a newly described aura known as secunda autem visio. It's not deja vu, which means already seen but ....'

'Second sight?' smiled Mr. Jenkins, anticipating the doctor's next words. 'What you are saying is that I have become psychic?'

'In a word, yes,' replied the GP. 'What you are perceiving when you have the epileptic fits is the reality behind the lies.'

'A form of extra-sensory perception?'

'Exactly.'

'Why should this have happened to me? asked the patient.

'There are several possible causes,' stated the GP. 'According to the YJM...'

'The Yak Journal of Medicine?'

'Quite...according to the journal it sometimes occurs spontaneously but it can rarely be due to trauma or tumour.' *Not quite as rarely as I'm suggesting.*

'So it could be due to a brain tumour?'

'In a minority of cases,' *and a whole load of other causes including vascular malformations, infection, previous febrile convulsions but he's right. Glioma is the most worrying.*

'OK doc,' replied the patient. 'When will I go for the scans?'

'They'll be arranged within two weeks as there is a risk of

cancer,' replied the GP. 'But I can put you on treatment today. About half of all new onset partial seizures are controlled effectively by the first drugs, either Carbamazepine or Lamotrigine.'

'Right,' agreed Mr. Jenkins. 'But would you mind if I delayed starting treatment for a few days?'

'No,' replied the GP. 'But why do you want to do that?'

'I want to buy a second-hand car and the second sight could be very useful,' answered the patient. 'Then I'll be happy to go on treatment. It can be so confusing knowing what people's hidden agendas and ulterior motives are.'

The doctor smiled as he wrote out the prescription. *Human beings cannot bear very much reality,* he thought as he did so.

'T.S. Eliot in Four Quartets,' said the patient as he took the script and waved goodbye.

NOTE

That was a fictional story but could almost be true. There are some conditions, such as Tourette' syndrome, that result in people saying unusual and often vulgar things but as far as I know "second sight" due to Temporal Lobe Epilepsy does not occur so don't go making that diagnosis just because you read about it here! The Yak Journal of Medicine is also imaginary.

So why did I write this story? I thought it would be interesting to point out the lies behind the advertisements and the media in general and to do so in the form of a parable.

Once I had decided that the second sight would be considered as an illness the idea of a variant of Temporal lobe epilepsy that causes secunda autem visio rather than deja vu was an obvious one. The rest of the story then fell into place.

Some people are better than others at detecting lies in the newspaper and in advertisements. Certainly second sight of that nature could prove very useful. Perhaps the fictional GP was being over zealous in wishing to treat it?

Frequently when I was a practising doctor I would attend committee meetings and sometimes, just sometimes, to enliven proceedings I would hide the meeting timetable in my jacket and then ask attendees if they would like to see my hidden agenda.....

Now how about a poem? This one was written after I had completed the anthology of poetry (Parables from Parallel Places: number one bestseller in the Poetry Anthology category, Amazon free downloads worldwide Christmas 2014).

People in my World

Bald headed men with gold rim glasses
Sitting around on their old age passes
Thinking they're from the upper classes
They should be shot

Middle aged ladies with greying hair
Walk through crowds as if they're not there
Out shopping as if life is a fair
Well it's not

Long haired students in torn tight trousers
Complain about the speed of internet browsers
But where are they when we need rabble rousers?
The lazy lot

Fat old men with great big bellies
Eating too much soup and jelly
Sit around watching endless telly
No wonder they become so smelly

It may take all sorts to make a world
But what a world we have got.

NOTE

After that cruel poem (please remember that I am a bald-headed, glasses-wearing OAP) we now move into the fantasy of the worlds of possible futures. Although ostensibly set in the time ahead this is fiction so the characters may also move into the present or the past.

The next story, *Predestined to Die*, introduces us to the future world of Mark and Harriet Caine. This world is explored further in the story that follows it, *A Sheitel for Burning*, in which we also make the acquaintance of infant prodigy, Charlie Caine. A passing reference is made to the Apleys who will feature in full length stories of their own which are outside the scope of this anthology.

Predestined to Die, and *A Sheitel for Burning* are science fiction rather than fantasy.

Predestined to Die

Islington, England 2039

'You can't be serious!' exclaimed Mark Caine.

The young barrister was staring at a brief brought in by his secretary. Barnsbury Chambers sounded fine as a name but there were no partners other than Caine and he was sited in the Caledonian Road, not in the more salubrious Barnsbury Square. There had been no work for weeks and the last few cases had been people trying to fight parking fines and various other petty traffic offences. Now, suddenly, out of the clear blue sky a murder case had emerged.

'The defendant specifically asked for you,' stated the secretary. 'The solicitor dealing with his case phoned earlier.'

'Right!' replied Caine, straightening his anachronistic tie.

Only very old fashioned people wore ties any more and a few professions. Barristers, with their wigs and gowns, were numbered among the latter.

Caine read through the details, scanning quickly but absorbing all the details with his near-eidetic ability.

'I've read about this in the papers,' he announced.

Again this was an anachronism. Nearly everybody read their news online. Mark, of course, did so when he felt like it but for enjoyment he still received one of the few paper editions. These were much slimmed down with only the précis of the news actually printed. There were no full size or even tabloid newspapers any more....just slim A4 magazines that carried the top stories which could then be accessed by waving a mobile cellphone over the page. This would then show more detail on the small screen or sync to any nearby computer with full details, readers comments, annotations, everything you might want.

Mark tended to read the paper version simply because there was too much detail online. He liked to think of himself as a busy man and that he did not have time to waste chasing up every cross reference that was thrown up by the plethora of hyperlinks.

In reality since he has set up on his own the work had been fitful at best. When he had been a junior in his previous chambers he had certainly been busy.... doing all the work of the seniors, the partners.

Right now he had no work on except the murder case. So take it he would even though he doubted very much that he was the right person for the job.

*

'So I was visited in my flat by my future self and told that I was going to commit a murder,' stated the vicar, the Reverend Andy Cartwright.

The man was dressed in a semi-casual manner with blue jeans and trainers but had on a white clerical collar against a dark blue shirt.... a dog collar was how Mark would have described it if asked.

'So you then blacked out and when you came round you had a gun in your hand and a dead physicist at your feet?'

'Right,' agreed Cartwright. 'And the dead man was the one that my future self had told me I was going to kill. Professor Holmberg.'

'Now I don't want to appear to be doubting your word but are you absolutely sure that the man you saw was your future self?' asked Caine.

'I hope it wasn't,' answered the cleric. 'But he looked exactly like me, right down to the same clothes. Mind you I am very short-sighted and I have to confess that I don't wear my glasses due to vanity.'

'You have never had your eyes lasered?'

'I'm too much of a coward though after this I think I might consider it.'

'After this?'

'When you get me off the charge,' mumbled the vicar. 'Obviously I am being set up and I didn't do it. I'm a pacifist.'

'But your future self?'

'May have been a fake. I don't want to accept the concept of time travel but he did sound like myself as well as look like me......'

Mark sat back. Here was a conundrum. If the vicar accepted the evidence of his own, admittedly myopic, eyes then time travel had occurred, he had been warned but had probably still killed the physicist. However, the vicar was not going to plead guilty since he had no first hand knowledge of killing the scientist.

'Then what happened?'

'The police arrived very quickly.'

'Did you call them?'

'I had no time and I did not know what to do. They found me standing there with a smoking gun.'

'Was it actually smoking?'

'I don't think so but the forensics all support that I did the crime according to my solicitor.'

'So the scientist was killed there and you were holding the gun?'

'True,' agreed the vicar. 'But I don't actually remember shooting the man.'

'Right,' Mark was puzzled.

What could he do as the barrister? Plead that the man was in a delusional state, believing he had seen himself? That seemed the best bet.

'Have you ever seen visions or heard voices?' asked Caine

'You are trying to determine whether I am sane or not,' nodded the priest. 'I understand your approach.'

'Well have you?'

'I'm sorry to say that the answer is no,' answered Cartwright. 'Many of my colleagues believe that God talks directly to them.'

'In a still small voice of calm,' added Caine.

'Indeed,' agreed the vicar. 'Just exactly that sort of thing. Whilst I believe that God could talk to me I have to tell you that, in all honesty, he has not done so.'

'Never?'

'Only through his word in the holy scriptures. Otherwise, no.'

'Now the physicist,' Mark decided to change the direction of his questioning.

Motive was the point since opportunity was clearly there.

'Yes?' queried the vicar.

'Did you have reason to hate him or wish him dead?'

'Some would say so,' stated Cartwright.

'Why? Can you elucidate?'

'Certainly,' agreed the vicar. 'I'm rather an old-fashioned type of vicar. I might wear jeans but I still wear the dog collar.

Yes, I know people call it that.'

Cartwright had noticed Mark's slight smile.

'But I try to keep up to date,' the vicar continued. 'I am quite well known via the media as I frequently give the *Thought for Today* on the radio.'

'That's where I heard you!' exclaimed Caine.

'And that is why I asked for you,' stated the priest. 'I must admit I thought that you would be older.'

'Why did you ask for me?'

'You wrote a letter to *Thought for Today* in response to one of my radio messages.'

Caine cast his mind back.

'So I did!' he exclaimed. 'I wrote in about a very thought-provoking talk. I felt I had to commend the speaker.'

'It was a talk about not despoiling the environment, about pollution and deforestation,' nodded the preacher. 'You agreed with everything I had said.'

'That's right,' Mark sat back contemplatively. 'But if that was the reason that you chose me I'm afraid that you may have made a bad choice.'

'Why?'

'Isn't it obvious?' asked Caine. 'My experience in cases like yours is very small.'

'You've been involved in numerous criminal cases including murder,' countered the vicar. 'I looked you up on the net.'

'I think you might have confused me with my father,' grimaced Caine. 'He was also called Mark Caine and had a huge practice and caseload. He was the defending barrister for many murder trials.'

'Then you can ask him for support and advice,' suggested Cartwright.

'Only if I can speak to him in the way that some of your vicar friends speak to God,' Mark sighed. 'I'm sorry to say that he died last year in a freak accident.'

'Perhaps you could use the time machine that seems to be at the heart of this problem,' suggested the priest.

'You must explain more,' demanded Caine, with an audible sigh. 'What time machine?'

'The dead physicist had invented a time machine and I had publicly debated with him whether or not it was ethical to use the machine.'

'Why would it not be ethical?'

'The physicist Holmberg and myself had several well publicised arguments. This culminated in the latest television debate which most people think was a success for the Professor,' it was the preacher's turn to sigh. 'I have to say that not everyone was of that opinion. My congregation was very supportive and told me that I had said the right things at the right time. If the majority of the public wanted to hear what Holmberg had to say and not what I said then that is up to them. It certainly did not upset me.'

'So you did not feel a murderous hatred towards him?' asked the young lawyer.

'Not at all,' answered the preacher. 'I did get rather heated during the debate but I am not a person who harbours grudges.'

'But you did think that time travel was unethical?' Caine was baffled.

Motivation was only there if the evangelist was upset with the scientist, thought Caine. *If he had been happy with the debates there was no obvious motive.*

'One thing that did come out of the debate was that I was

convinced by the Professor that he had experimental evidence of time travel,' explained Reverend Cartwright. 'Before that I had thought that his ideas had been purely theoretical but there was no doubt that it had gone a lot further than I thought. I am not alone in believing that the ethics of science need to be thought out before the experimentation. I am sure you realise that?'

'I do,' agreed Caine. 'Too many times scientists have gone on their merry way believing that the pursuit of knowledge should have no bounds, unconcerned where that knowledge might lead. Nuclear bombs, lead in petrol, CFCs.'

'Exactly!' exclaimed the clergyman. 'You do understand my point.'

'But in this case, specifically....'

'It may interfere with the very nature of time itself,' the priest shook his head sorrowfully. 'I must say that I found Professor Holmberg's can-do and will-do attitude repugnant. His arrogance was overbearing.'

'What was your main concern with regards to time travel?'

'Holmberg laughed at me and implied that they could travel back in time and prove that the bible was wrong,' stated Reverend Cartwright. 'But that was not my concern at all. I'm convinced that it is right....well, the New Testament and in particular the Gospels are right.'

'So what was your concern?'

'In the book of Romans, Chapter eight and verse twenty-nine, it says *"For those God foreknew he also predestined to be conformed to the image of his Son,"* and in Ephesians *"In him we have obtained an inheritance, having been predestined according to the purpose",*' stated the vicar, quoting the verses without need of any text.

'I don't quite see the point....' replied Caine.

'Surely you understand?' the vicar questioned Caine. 'Isn't it obvious? With a time machine you could constantly go back and forwards interfering with the destiny which God determined from the moment of creation. A time machine could interfere with the Almighty's divine and already determined plan.'

'Unless the time machine was already part of the plan?' suggested Caine.

'I see your point,' agreed the vicar. 'But changing the past could set up paradoxes threatening the present and it is God's prerogative to know the future, not man's.'

'Could you possibly have killed the physicist in order to save humanity from making what in your eyes would be a grave mistake?'

'If I did kill the man that would have been the only reason,' replied the priest. 'But I still do not really believe that I did do it.'

'But you think you saw your future self?'

'Yes I do, but surely that was a hoax?'

'Why would someone try to hoax you in that way?' asked Caine.

'You'd have to ask whoever did it,' suggested the vicar.

*

'This is a clearcut case, my Lord,' the prosecution were putting the worst possible picture of the situation, summing up near the end of the trial. 'The doors were locked and bolted from the inside, the defendant had the gun in his hand and the victim was lying at his feet. We have put the evidence forward and rest our case. The Reverend Cartwright is guilty of murder most foul.'

The prosecuting barrister sat down.

The trial was being heard in the Central Criminal Court of England and Wales known as the Old Bailey. Built on the site of the old Newgate gaol it had been destroyed twice.... once in the fire of London in 1666, rebuilt 1674, and secondly in the cataclysms that occurred when Parsifal X had tried to combine the parallel realities. The present building had reopened in 2025.

'Thank you,' replied the judge. 'And what does the defense have to say?'

Mark's case had gone rather badly to start with. He had addressed the judge as 'Your Honour' but the old buffer had responded by saying that he could not hear him. It took Caine some time to realise that the judge was not deaf, merely refusing to listen because the correct way of addressing the fellow in the Old Bailey was My Lord or My Lady. When Mark had realised his gaffe things had improved but the evidence was strikingly bad. All of the forensic science pointed to just one culprit. The doors were locked, the windows closed, the gun in Cartwright's hand and the physicist was dead, killed by a bullet from the gun. The gun was an old-fashioned hand gun with explosive bullets and the only slight discrepancy was with the powder burns. If the physicist had been shot at point-blank range there should have been obvious burns on the victim's clothes from the hot gases that were expelled from the muzzle of the firearm. There were none. The prosecution had dismissed this by saying that the vicar could easily have been standing further back in the room when he took a shot at the scientist.

'My Lord,' started Mark and the judge nodded. 'The evidence presented has all been circumstantial. The major flaws in the prosecution's case are these. The Reverend did not own a gun, had never fired one in his life and therefore had no ability to shoot the physicist from the other side of the room. He had no motive for such a crime and the prosecution has failed to address the incident of the visit to the clergyman of his future self just before the murder.'

'And what are your thoughts about this future apparition?' asked the judge, talking in a more kindly manner.

'I believe that it was a hoaxer, my Lord,' replied Caine. 'And I actually think that it might have been the person who did the murder.'

'I object, my Lord,' cried the prosecuting counsel. 'If that were the case where was the man when the police arrived to a locked room murder?'

'Objection sustained,' replied the judge. 'Mister Caine kindly keep your remarks pertinent. Do you have any further comments to make?'

'I would like to ask for an adjournment, my Lord,' replied Mark Caine, barrister at law. 'I wish to bring a further witness but he is not with us presently.'

'And who would that witness be?' asked the judge.

'I have come to believe that time travel is relevant to this case and the witness I wish to call is Mr. Karl Raven, the chief investor in the dead scientist's research project.'

'I object, my Lord,' cried the prosecuting counsel. 'The question of time travel has no bearing on the case.'

'I disagree,' stated the judge. 'If there was no successful invention of a time travelling machine there would be no motive for the defendant to murder the physicist. So your objection is overruled. You may call your extra witness, Mr. Caine, but in future I would like to point out that it is customary to present the entirety of your case, including all the witnesses, before you sum up. We shall meet tomorrow at eleven am.'

'Thank you my Lord,' replied Caine.

*

'Why did you want to call Karl Raven?' asked the evangelist when Caine was visiting him in his cell later that day.

'You were doomed if I didn't do something replied Caine. 'I was watching the reaction of the jury and to a man they had you marked down as guilty.'

'But I really don't think that I would have done it,' the priest was hesitant. 'Unless he had really riled me and I had thought the world would be better off without the man. Even then I would have thought that it was up to God to decide.'

'Locked room, gun in hand,' stated Caine. 'Totally damning. The only way out was to pursue another witness so I plumped for the investor.'

'Chase the money!' exclaimed the vicar, brightening up. 'That was one of your father's maxims. Go where the money goes.'

'Yes,' agreed Caine. 'Chase the money.'

I wish it was as simple as that, thought Caine. *In reality I wanted to delay things but my father was usually right. I must chase the money.*

*

Burning the midnight oil looking at the internet had convinced Caine that his father might indeed be right.

By two a.m. he *knew* his old Pa was correct. The money was at the root of all this. But how and why?

Karl Raven was a very famous wealth management consultant but in this particular project he had invested a veritable fortune. The net told him that one of the major investors, via Raven's firm, was Roger Clay, an East End gangster. If the investment had gone wrong the gangster would have been a formidable foe for Raven to contend with.

Perhaps the physicist's machine did not work? If that were the case he might have needed to convince the world of the opposite.

No, that was surely too far fetched.

Then why the masquerade as the future clergyman? Unless the future self was real and the vicar really had committed murder.... that was, of course, the easy explanation.

Caine worked on through the night following the chain of information and pseudo-information that the internet threw up. How much was true and how much was false he could not easily determine but he was building up a picture about Karl Raven, his investment empire and the sort of clients that he worked for and with.

*

'You are Karl Raven, investment manager?' asked Caine.

'Guilty as accused,' smiled the financier, with a slight laugh.

'Mr. Raven,' the judge spoke in a severe manner. 'Your attitude is too lighthearted. This is the Central Criminal Court of Justice for the whole of England and Wales. You are not a stand up comedian and this is not Live at the Palladium.'

What the heck is that? wondered Caine.

'Could you enlighten us about the nature of your investment in the victim's research and tell us something about the research itself?' Caine asked the witness.

'Certainly,' replied the financier, speaking in a much more serious tone. 'Professor Holmberg had invented a working time machine. Chrono-spatial displacement is what he called it.'

'And you have seen this working?' asked the judge, leaning forward, clearly focussed and interested in the statement from the witness. 'You have actually seen things displaced in time and space?'

'Only small objects, your honour,' replied the witness.

The judge did not correct Raven's form of address.

'So large living objects like people could not be moved in time?' asked the judge.

'I did not see that happen but Holmberg told me that he had travelled in time repeatedly, to the past and to the future.'

'So Reverend Cartwright could have travelled back to visit himself and warn him to not admit the physicist to his premises or he would end up killing him?'

The judge had taken over the questioning and the answers were not going the way that Caine had hoped. Reverend Cartwright was sitting with his head in his hands, hiding his face from view.

'Yes, your honour,' agreed Raven.

'Do you have any further questions of the witness?' the judge was asking Caine.

He shook his head in reply. The judge repeated his question, now directing it to the prosecution.

'No, my lord,' replied the counsel.

'Then I....' the judge started to pronounce but Caine interrupted.

'Actually I do have a question,' asked Caine then added, rather belatedly. 'My Lord.'

'Go ahead Mr. Caine,' the judge replied resignedly.

'It is a simple question,' stated Caine, looking as severe as he could and speaking directly to the witness. 'Why were you lying to us? What you said was a tissue of lies but why?'

'What, me?' blustered Raven. 'Lying, in what way? When?'

'I object your honour,' shouted the Crown Prosecutor. 'That question was irrelevant, immaterial and irrational.'

Just like an old Perry Mason programme, thought Caine. *My father loved them.*

'Objection overruled,' replied the judge. 'I'm rather keen to see where Caine is going with this.'

'If the court would not mind, my Lord, I would like to explain why it is firstly impossible for Cartwright to have been visited by himself and secondly untrue that the physicist repeatedly travelled into the past and into the future.'

'OK,' agreed the judge. 'Go ahead.'

'Firstly visiting himself. The Reverend stated that the person who looked like him was dressed in the same clothes that he was wearing, including the dog collar and had come from the near future back in time to warn him that he would kill the physicist if he let him into the premises.'

'Yes Mr, Caine. We have all heard that. What do you have to tell us that is new?' the judge spoke testily, perhaps regretting allowing Caine to continue.

'Well he couldn't do that since he would be locked up, my Lord' stated Caine. 'Don't you see? There was no time for his future self to travel back in time.'

'Why not immediately after shooting the man?' asked the judge. 'Then the defendant from the future could have collapsed with the gun in his hand.'

'Two things make that unlikely,' remarked Caine. 'Did he have the gun in his hand when he arrived back from the future? I think not or the Reverend would have told us so. And the time was too short for the defendant to have travelled to the physicist's laboratory, learnt how to work the machine and then arrived back to warn himself.'

'I see the point. How do you answer that?' asked the judge, addressing Raven who was still stood in the witness box.

'I'm not the one who said he was visited by himself,' blustered Raven. 'That was the defendant.'

'OK,' continued Mark. 'So you have no actual answer to that conundrum. It could not have been the vicar because the police came very quickly and locked him up and he has not been free since to travel in time..... and if he is guilty he will not be free for a very long time.'

'Did you have another point?' asked the judge.

'This is even more of a problem, my Lord,' stated Caine.

'Go ahead.'

'If the victim, Holmberg the physicist, were able to travel in time into the future and into the past, why could he not predict his own death or prevent it?'

'It might have been inevitable,' interrupted the prosecution counsel. 'And in any case I object, my Lord!'

'Objection overruled. Continue Mr. Caine.'

'If it was inevitable why did he not tell people who his murderer was going to be?' Caine paused after directing the question to Raven.

Raven was becoming very flustered and red in the face before he eventually replied.

'Because he told me that the machine did cause an element of amnesia,' the financier felt he was getting onto firmer ground. 'That would explain why the Reverend was not able to remember killing the physicist.'

'I don't think that is at all likely,' countered Caine. 'If Professor Holmberg had contracted amnesia every occasion he travelled in time he would have realised that it was a problem. From then on he could simply take a pencil and paper with him when he went time travelling and write down what happened.'

'They couldn't take pencils through the machine as the graphite caused a short circuit,' the financier was really sweating.

'Then a pen, perhaps?' asked Caine, raising an eyebrow.

'They burst due to the heating effect,' confabulated Raven.

'Chalk?'

'Exploded!'

'Wax crayon?'

'Melted.'

'And yet human beings, mostly carbon and water just like graphite and ink, were unharmed?'

'It's surprising but that is the effect,' stated the financier.

'But it's not, is it?' asked Caine.

'I object,' cried the prosecutor.

'Yes,' said the judge. 'Why do you flatly contradict the witness. Do you have other evidence?'

'I do, my Lord,' Caine nodded his head and lifted a pile of printed paper. 'These are patents awarded to Professor Holmberg referring to the time machine.'

Caine lifted another pile of similar pages.

'And these are scientific papers published in online journals right up until eight o'clock this morning, my Lord.'

'And what do they show?' asked the judge.

'They show that chrono-spatial displacement does occur due to the machine, my Lord, but the largest object displaced was a bottle of wine. Nothing larger than that has been possible with the machinery described.'

'That's interesting,' agreed the judge. 'What do you say to that?'

The judge leant over and stared at the witness. Raven went red again and the sweat poured off his brow.

'We, er, we have a much bigger machine in a secret location,' he finally stammered.

'Which the defendant serendipitously found?' queried the judge. 'You would, of course, be happy to divulge the whereabouts of this larger machine to the court.'

'It is highly secret, your honour,' retorted Raven. 'It is a trade secret and we have to beware of industrial sabotage.'

'So you wouldn't like us to see the machine?' the judge raised his eyebrows in mock horror and surprise.

Caine stood to talk again.

'What I think happened, my Lord, is that Raven discovered that you could shoot a bullet through the machine and somehow was able to guide it forward or back in time such that it struck Professor Holmberg when he was at the Reverend's flat.'

'That's ridiculous,' cried the investment manager. 'Why would I do that?'

'Perhaps you had promised your investors something more than a machine that prematurely aged bottles of wine?' suggested Caine. 'In particular Roger Clay might not have been happy, I imagine.'

'Why shouldn't he have been happy?' squeaked the financier.

'Because you have been promising everybody a huge machine that can move people back to see their dead loved ones and forwards to see the winner at the Epsom Derby!' exclaimed Caine. 'And the biggest object that could be moved is a bottle of wine and all the animals experimented on perished.'

'I have done no such thing,' protested the ragged investment manager. 'I always deliver what I promise. I wouldn't promise things without a good reason.'

'You had a good reason, that's the point,' Caine waved his hand at the witness. 'You were told by the physicist that the machine would work perfectly. You gathered investors to the tune of four billion pounds and then discovered that the physicist was lying. He could not move people, only objects.'

'But why would I kill him before he could rectify his mistake?' asked Raven.

'Because the guy thought that it was some immutable fact of nature related to Heisenberg's principle of uncertainty,' summarised Caine, pointing to the pile of papers. 'It was all there in his scientific papers and he was about to tell the Reverend that he did not need to worry about the ethics, time travel as he had imagined it was only for inanimate objects not for the living.'

'So why did the Reverend think he saw himself?' asked the judge, slightly alarmed and confused by the turn around in the evidence.

'Raven impersonated him, my Lord,' stated Caine. 'The vicar wears easily copied clothes and Raven looks vaguely like the Reverend. I expect that a search of his home would reveal a dark blue shirt and white clerical collar.'

'I still don't understand how an intelligent man could be fooled like that?' queried the judge.

'Raven must have slipped something into the vicar's tea, perhaps Rohypnol?' suggested Caine. 'Blood was taken from Cartwright when he was arrested but has not been tested for toxicology.'

'That would be interesting,' agreed the judge. 'But why would Raven need to go to Cartwright's place at all?'

'Probably to call the physicist over to speak to the Reverend and to place something on the chair so that the bullet from the past would fly through the physicist.'

'So who could have locked the door from the inside, Mr. Clever Dick?' cried Raven.

'The physicist, of course,' replied Caine. 'When you phoned him, posing as Cartwright, you gave poor Professor Holmberg strict instructions about letting himself in and sitting in a particular place in the hallway to wait for the Reverend, who you were pretending to be, to come out of his room. Little did the poor man know that by sitting there he was sealing his own doom.'

'The case does stack up well. What do you say to all of this Mr. Raven?' asked the judge.

'It's all rubbish!' screamed the financier, looking manically at all of the people in the courtroom. 'You can't believe this tissue of lies. How come the Reverend was found with the gun in his hand?'

'That was pushed through the time machine too and the vicar picked it up from the floor in his confused and drugged state. It was your fortune that he did so but your murderous ruse has been discovered.'

Karl Raven suddenly jumped up from his seat and leapt from the dock. He ran full pelt at Caine.

'You fool,' he cried, clawing at the barrister. 'You've doomed me. Now Clay will be after me and my life will be forfeit.'

'I've already spoken to the police about Clay,' sighed Caine. 'They've been trying to find out how he was laundering his money for a very long time. They were extremely grateful for the information.'

The investment manager stared wildly around then ran towards the entrance where he was wrestled to the ground by the sergeant at arms.

'Arrest that man,' cried the judge.

Raven was being taken away, struggling hard against the handcuffs placed on him by the court police, as Caine spoke again.

'In the light of the events I would humbly ask, my Lord, that the case against my client be dismissed.'

'I object,' cried the prosecuting counsel, rather feebly and aware of his weak position.

'Case of the Crown against Reverend Andrew Cartwright dismissed,' cried the judge, hitting his gavel on the wooden block.

Andy Cartwright looked as if he could not believe his ears. His face was beaming with smiles.

*

'How did you know that I didn't do it?' asked the Reverend as they sat drinking tea together in the chambers on Caledonian Road. 'I was even worried that I might have done it myself.'

'I didn't know,' replied Caine. 'But I figured that anyone so shortsighted that they could believe someone impersonating them was really their future self had to be both drugged and incapable of shooting straight.'

'Amazing,' the Reverend shook his head. 'You'll better your father's reputation yet.'

'Thank you,' replied Caine. 'But what amazed me was that Raven did not understand the value of what he actually had. A working time machine, however small, is an astonishing achievement. I phoned several physicists early today before the court was sitting and any of them would have given their eyeteeth for such a machine. There is no need for human beings to be sent travelling in time, small robots could do the job. They could record videos, take samples. Living tissue and a huge machine were not necessary.'

'So Raven could have got all his money back?'

'Plus some, easily,' replied Caine. 'The murder was completely unnecessary.'

'As is all violence,' concluded the vicar.

NOTE

Predestined to die is classical science fiction and was originally written by myself nearly twenty years ago. It has been extensively rewritten and abridged for this anthology. The next story continues in the same sci fi vein. It is fairly long as short stories go (about 10,000 words) and may therefore qualify as a novelette! In fact it is so long that I felt obliged to break it into chapters.

A Sheitel for Burning

Prologue

'I will lift up mine eyes unto the mountains; From whence shall my help come?

My help cometh from the Lord, Who made heaven and earth.

He will not suffer thy foot to be moved; He that keepeth thee will not slumber.

Behold, He that keepeth Israel doth neither slumber nor sleep.'

Reading these words from the psalms Benjamin Higgs sprinkled the ashes of his beloved wife on the sacred lower slopes of the Mount of Olives, just east of Old Jerusalem.

Chapter 1

Bristol, England May 2043

The sun was beating down from an azure blue sky and it was days like this that made Mark Caine think that he was living in the most beautiful spot on the planet. That was as long as he was able to forget the the four solid months of rain over the winter and a sky that looked like the inside of a tupperware box.

Now, however, it was delightful, sunny and warm. They were planning to fly over to their holiday home in Montemar, near Malaga in Spain just for the weekend. It would be little Charlie's third birthday so Mark and Harriet intended putting on a party for him during the afternoon of Saturday the 16th.

Charlie knew he was coming up to his third birthday and was counting down the days to his party. In fact he was a prodigy and was regaling his father with the exact number of hours, minutes and seconds before he reached the age of three.

It's no surprise really, thought Mark. *Harriet's an astonishing woman. A freelance journalist and broadcaster and gifted computer hacker.* All this and she had still agreed to marry him after their whirlwind romance in the aftermath of the Cartwright Case, the so-called "Time Travel Murder".

The Reverend Doctor Andrew Cartwright had been the priest who conducted their marriage service in the Caledonian Road Baptist Church and had blessed their union. Much to their mutual delight it was a blessing that had proved fruitful just ten months after the wedding.

Harriet and Mark were both still working. Following the

success of the Cartwright Case, Mark had been in great demand internationally. Harriet had been a sympathetic journalist who, from the start, had refused to believe that the Reverend Doctor should be vilified in the way that the other media had portrayed him. Her career, already very successful, had flourished.

The couple had decided to move to Bristol which was close to where Mark had been born. Although initially famous as a criminal law advocate Mark had chosen to move his career in a different direction. In private he was happy to admit that he had not enjoyed the mauling in court that he had received when representing the defence in the Cartwright Case. He and Harriet now worked together closely in a business law practice: investigating insurance claims, undertaking due diligence for very large companies involved in takeovers and arranging the contracts for huge financial deals.

None of this could have happened without the enormous publicity around the "Time Travel Murder". This had been enhanced by Harriet's part-time occupation as Vanessa, the intrepid reporter for Channel 195 Live.

As well as a live-in nanny they were able to afford the assistance of a part-time cleaner and a gardener. Best of all Mark's mother was a delighted grandma living just a few miles away.

Mark had to admit it...things were going well!

*

'A new case,' Harriet waved some papers at Mark as he sat on the grass playing with Charlie.

'What is it love?' asked Mark, looking first at his lady and then up at an ominous cloud that had formed in the sky above them.

'A big one. Kidnapping insurance,' replied Harriet. 'The insurance company would like us to investigate. You can do the legal work whilst I look into the kidnapping aspect.'

'We've been steering clear of criminal cases,' Mark was just a little worried. 'Do you think it's wise to get involved?'

Plit-plat. Sure enough it had started to rain. They gathered up the playthings and went indoors.

'You'll find this one interesting,' Harriet grinned. 'It's the Higgs case.'

'Higgs as in the boson or Higgs as in the multi-billionaire?' asked Caine.

'It must be the rich one Daddy,' shouted the almost-three year old Charlie, jumping up and down as he said it.

'Why did you say that?' asked Caine, intrigued by his precocious child.

'Everyone knows about the Higgs boson, silly,' replied the kid. 'But you can't kidnap an elementary particle.'

'No, you're right,' agreed Caine ruefully.

Not for the first time he found that his child was just a bit spooky, the things he could do at such an early age! Why couldn't he seem to play like other kids? Other kids, that is, who had not had their brains super-wired with bio-compatible electronic chips. They were much like Charlie but Charlie did it without brain enhancement. Damned spooky.

'He's right,' agreed Harriet. 'It's the billionaire.'

'He has been kidnapped?' Caine was intrigued. 'He's having a bit of a rotten time. It's not long since his wife died.'

'You're right,' agreed Harriet. 'But it's not Benjamin Higgs himself who has been kidnapped. It's his wife's twin sister.'

'You're going to have to tell me the whole story,' Caine was reconciling himself with the idea of taking on the case.

Harriet sat back to explain the background.

'As you know Maureen Higgs died six months ago after a long debilitating illness,' Harriet looked at Caine and he nodded so she continued the narrative. 'What you will not have heard is that one week ago Higgs received a ransom demand from somebody purporting to be the person who had kidnapped Rebecca Cohen twenty-five years ago.'

'Twenty-five years ago?' Caine was astonished. 'That's surely a tall story? How could she have been kept captive all that time?'

'Difficult to imagine,' agreed Harriet. 'But it has happened before. Carlina White of Harlem, for example, also known as Netty Nance. She was kidnapped as a baby and solved her own case twenty-three years later in 2011.'

'That was the USA not England.'

'True,' agreed Harriet. 'They're usually murdered in the UK.' Caine winced.

'Any others?'

'Going further back, Cynthia Ann Parker was kidnapped by Commanches, lived with them for twenty-four years and married a war chief.'

'That's the USA again and must have been much further back.'

'Sure,' agreed Harriet. 'It was in 1836. There have been quite a few children who were kidnapped for ten years or so and then eventually released alive.'

'But twenty-five years would be the longest?'

'Probably, although it is hard to know since there were 140,000 reports of missing children in the UK per year back at the time that Rebecca went missing.'

'Which would have been in 2018 by simple arithmetic,'

Caine nodded. 'But these days the camera surveillance and the implanted chips have reduced the number of cases dramatically?'

'Absolutely,' agreed Harriet. 'And even Rebecca's abduction should have been recorded by the family's security cameras but they were turned off at the time. An inside job was suspected but never proven.'

'And she was declared dead after seven years?'

'Quite right. The ransom demand was a considerable surprise for Benjamin Higgs. He had never even met Rebecca.'

'Her sister Maureen was quite famous in her time,' Mark Caine reminisced. 'She was a very prominent heiress.'

'Very rich indeed, heiress to the largest grocery chain in England.'

'So where do we come in to the picture?'

'KNR International, Kidnap and Ransom Insurance company would like us to investigate.'

'How much is the ransom demand?'

'Two billion pounds sterling.'

'Whewwwee,' Caine whistled. 'That is an impressive amount. How much of that would be covered by the insurance?'

'The insurance only provides cover up to five hundred million pounds.'

'Only?' Mark queried the use of the term.

'It's only a quarter of the amount, Daddy,' piped up the diminutive Charlie, who had been listening to all of the story. 'Benjamin Higgs would have to provide one and a half billion pounds. That's still a lot of money.'

Charlie's grasp of the situation once again amazed Mark. The kid was not yet three and he was pointing out problems like a pro!

'Certainly I can see that they might want us to be involved with that sort of sum involved,' agreed Caine. 'What exactly do they want us to do?'

'Arrange the transfer of the money if it comes to it,' replied Harriet, picking up the wonder-kid and a giving him a big hug as she said it. 'And check that Higgs has sufficient for his side of the bargain.'

'Won't it cripple the insurance company?'

'It will represent a major loss to them this year but they reckon that they will receive huge numbers of new subscribers when it all goes viral from the Channel 195 Live channel.'

'Subscribers to their kidnap and ransom policies?'

'Of course,' agreed Harriet. 'If Rebecca is returned unharmed it would represent the biggest kidnapping and successful return story of the century and the company would eventually do very well out of the deal.'

'Does Higgs really have sufficient money to make up the sum?'

'He's the chairman of HMJ-WM,' declared Harriet. 'Higgs, Martin and Jones Investment and Wealth Management.'

'And they are undoubtedly huge.'

'The biggest in the UK,' Harriet concurred. 'He certainly has enough money to pay his part.'

*

'Mum?' asked Charlie later the same afternoon. 'What would happen if I was kidnapped?'

'We would set out and find you,' answered Harriet. 'And get you back.'

'But what if they took me somewhere that you couldn't find me?' asked the little boy. 'I'm not chipped so you couldn't find me that way.'

'If you had your mobile on you we could trace that,' answered Harriet.

'Unless they kept me in a shielded room,' stated the smart kid. 'Then what would you do?'

'If we couldn't find you I suspect you would have to free yourself,' replied the boy's mother. 'You're very clever. You could find a way.'

'Like Spiderman and the Goblin?' asked Charlie. 'Could I use superpowers?'

'If you had them,' answered his mother. 'But your superpower is your intelligence. That's what would keep you safe.'

She picked up the little fellow. For all his precocious abilities he was still only a tiny mite. She squeezed him tightly, then kissed him and put him back on the grass. It was getting time for tea so they would soon have to go inside. There were still some preparations to make for the boy's birthday party.

*

'Happy birthday to you, Happy birthday to you.'

They were all gathered round singing to Charlie who was sat like a king listening to his courtiers. He was dressed in a brand new blue suit and had a pair of patent leather shoes with silver buckles. He had chosen the shoes himself and was very proud of them.

Five little children varying in age from nearly three to six were sat round singing and playing with Charlie. It was not a large gathering as the holiday flat was just over a thousand miles from Bristol. However Charlie had endeared himself to the local people in Montemar and four children had come from the local surrounds,

The youngest child was Arkon Apley who was just under three. He had flown in with his parents all the way from

Toronto. They were staying at the Caine's apartment for a full three weeks something about which Mark was slightly jealous since Harriet, Charlie and himself could only afford the weekend away because work beckoned. If the Higgs case had not turned up they could at least have stayed for the week. Arkon's brother Andover had not been able to come as he was away on a field trip from secondary school.

The kid who perturbed Mark was Jennifer Reynolds, an English girl who lived locally. Her parents were computer programmers and she had been maximally implanted with chips soon after birth. She was slightly older than little Charlie but talked like someone who was middle-aged and already knew far too much about life. Whereas Charlie's talent was inherent hers was artificial and world weary.

Jennifer was, for once, joining in the fun with everyone else.

Having just had the cake-cutting ceremony they would be eating a piece each followed by some quiet games and then musical chairs and a game of balloon volley ball.

'Do you think you can save Rebecca?'

It was a quiet moment in the party and Charlie's friends had run off following an errant ball. The three-year old asked the question of his mother very earnestly.

'You don't need to worry about it, Charlie boy,' replied Harriet, tousling his hair.

'Well,' he said very sagely for such a young child. 'That is a huge amount of money and people would do a lot of bad things for so much money. You and Daddy couldn't earn that much in a thousand years.'

Mark Caine was listening to the conversation whilst keeping an eye on the other children. Once again the precocity of his child almost scared him. For surely Charlie was right? It was a huge sum of money and people had done terrible things for much less money. Much less money indeed.

*

'We've come to chat to you about the ransom demand,' explained Mark Caine quietly to the immaculately dressed chairman of the wealth management firm HMJ-WM.

They were sat in the board room of the wealth management company in London where Benjamin Higgs had asked them to meet him. Higgs looked Harriet and Caine up and down critically.

'I'm told you are the best that money can buy,' he finally stated. 'And that the two of you have been successful in the insurance investigation field?'

'This is true,' agreed Harriet.

'I'm assuming that you have experience in negotiating ransom payments?' Higgs added this almost as an after thought.

'Not as much experience because such demands are rare these days,' admitted Caine. 'Tracers, chips, surveillance cameras, satellite images. All of these have made kidnapping more difficult.'

'But this kidnapping occurred long ago,' declared Higgs. 'And the ransom demand has only just surfaced.'

'We will need to go over all of the background with you,' stated Harriet. 'But first things first. We have brought our terms and conditions of engaging our services for you to spend time reading.'

To Harriet's surprise the man signed the forms without a second glance.

'Now ask away!' he demanded whilst sitting back in his chair with his hands clenched behind his head and his elbows sticking out to each side.

'To start with we need to know what was in the ransom note, how it came to you and where the person obtained your address,' stated Mark. 'And the circumstances around your sister-in-law's disappearance.'

'OK,' the financier was almost falling off his chair he was so stretched out and relaxed. 'I'll start at the top. Rebecca, my wife's twin, went missing almost precisely twenty-five years ago.'

'What was the background to her disappearance?' asked Harriet.

'From what I understand,' started the financier. 'And don't forget this is all hearsay, since I was not around at the time.'

Mark and Harriet nodded to urge the financier on.

'What I understand as the facts of the case,' Higgs leant forward a little. 'Is that Rebecca was the slightly more beautiful of the two girls.'

'I thought that they were identical twins?' queried Mark, surprised that this should have been the first piece of information that Higgs thought worth imparting.

'My wife, Maureen, was, of course, very beautiful but people have told me confidentially that Rebecca had a little bit more of a spark,' explained Higgs. 'So when she went missing they thought it was high jinks. That she was staying with a friend, something of that nature.'

'So there were no signs of a break-in, a struggle or anything like that?' asked Harriet.

'None at all,' answered Higgs. 'My in-laws told me that their memory of the occasion was very vivid. Indeed, so was that of my wife.'

'Are we able to to talk to your wife's parents?' asked Caine.

'Not unless you use a medium,' replied Higgs. 'They died in the shuttle crash two years ago.'

'And your wife is unfortunately deceased?' asked Caine, knowing the answer to be in the affirmative but wishing to hear it from the man himself.

'Yes,' Higgs answered with a sigh. 'Dead and buried. Or more correctly I should say scattered.'

'OK,' Harriet wanted to steer the conversation back to the period when the girl went missing. 'When she disappeared did they say anything else was strange?'

'Two things. The first is that the cameras were off. This was extraordinary and appeared to have been instigated by Rebecca herself. Certainly her code was used.'

'And the other?'

'Her cards went with her but none of her favourite clothes, shoes or other articles.'

'Did she use the cards?' Harriet cross questioned.

'Just once at a petrol station outside town the same day,' replied Higgs. 'Which was one of the reasons that they thought it was just high jinks. But when they were not used again and she never returned it was assumed that the kidnapper had forced her to use the cards and then murdered her.'

'No video surveillance at the gas station?' Caine asked this.

'There was but the images were blurred. The person who used the pay-at-the-pump facility had a hood over his or her head obscuring the face. And that was the last sighting of Rebecca, if it was her, and the last that was ever heard of the girl until the ransom note.'

'So what exact age was she when she went missing?' asked Harriet.

'Seventeen,' replied Higgs, shifting a little in his chair as if he was becoming impatient.

'Just a few more questions,' suggested Caine.

'Of course, of course,' replied Higgs.

'Do you think that this is a hoaxer who is simply after your money?' asked the lawyer. 'Or do you have reason to believe that the contact is genuine?'

'That question has been going through my mind,' answered the financier. 'I have the note here. Perhaps forensic science can tell if it is genuine.'

Higgs passed a typed paper note over to Caine, commenting as he did so.

'On paper,' Higgs stated. 'So that it would be harder to trace, I expect. I understand that even the best encrypted and anonymous electronic message can be partially if not fully traced.'

Mark and Harriet looked at the short note.

May 12th

I have Rebecca Cohen

She is too old to amuse me now. If you would like her as a replacement for your dead wife you must pay £2 billion. More details to follow but indicate willingness to trade by a short open video on DueTube under your normal name and entitled exactly "25 years but now too old".

If there is no reply within seven days of receipt of this letter I will assume that you wish me to dispose of her.

El Secuestrador

'Have many people touched this?' asked Harriet.

'My butler and myself,' answered Higgs. 'It arrived at home by post. My butler opened the letter and gave it to me.'

'And the envelope?'

'He had already destroyed it,' replied Higgs. 'When I read the letter I instantly called him but he had put the envelope in the instant recycling chute.'

'Did he not understand the significance of keeping the evidence?' asked Harriet, amazed at this turn of events.

'He did not read the letter,' explained the financier. 'It was folded over like so.'

Higgs folded the paper in three and on the other side they could see the words.

Private, for the eyes of Benjamin Higgs only.

'Yes, I understand,' nodded Harriet. 'have you shown this to the police?'

'Look young lady,' Benjamin Higgs was becoming very impatient. 'Have the insurance company not given you the full details? I gave them all the information.'

'We have to hear it for ourselves,' replied Harriet, pointing to her bag as she spoke. 'I have a full file on this already but your nuances are important. What about the police?'

'The police have not been involved as yet as I do not know whether or not this is simply a hoax brought on by my wife's death,' the financier sighed loudly. 'Goodness knows I have had plenty of charity requests, distant relatives and hangers-on getting in touch and this seemed to be just another one with a disturbing twist.'

'And an enormous amount of money demanded,' replied Caine. 'I don't suppose that the other requests amounted to anything like this sum.'

'To you,' replied Higgs with a rather superior tilt to his head.

'Two billion pounds may seem like an enormous sum.'

'It does,' agreed Caine readily.

'But to me it does not,' answered the multi-billionaire. 'Do you have any idea how much money HMJ-WM manages?'

'Several billion pounds sterling?' suggested Mark.

The financier laughed at the estimate.

'At the last count we were handling three trillion US dollars. That is three with twelve noughts after it.'

'Yes, I know what a trillion is,' replied Caine, just a little testily. 'One million million. Unless you happen to be in a long scale country in which case it is a million times greater.'

'Do we know which country the demand came from?' asked Harriet. 'It's interesting that the demand is in pounds. If it was one of the long scale countries two billion might mean ten times more, thus equalling twenty billion dollars on our short scale.'

'The butler did happen to notice that the postmark was from Gibraltar,' replied Higgs, less amused now. 'That is still effectively a sterling zone.'

'So a short scale,' remarked Caine. 'Did he notice anything else.'

'Not really but you are welcome to come to our house and question him,' replied Higgs. 'The only people who know about this are the butler and KNR International, the Kidnap and Ransom Insurance company.'

'What about your children?'

'They will have to hear about it if you decide that a money transfer should be arranged,' replied Higgs. 'They are major shareholders in HMJ-WM but up till now I have kept them out of this. They obviously never met their Auntie Rebecca. She disappeared long before they were born.'

'What about the other shareholders?' asked Harriet.

'It's a family firm,' answered Higgs. 'There are no other shareholders.'

'Would you be selling shares to raise the money?' asked Caine. 'I presume that the investors' money is ring-fenced.'

'Of course,' answered Higgs testily. 'This would be coming out of the shareholders' capital account not the clients' account.'

'Right,' replied Caine. 'I get it but does that amount of money sit in the shareholders' capital account?'

'Of course not,' replied the financier. 'We would have to liquidate some assets but that could be done very quickly. We may need to sell some shares. Discretion and absolute secrecy is vital or it could affect their value'

'Caine and I will have to discuss this,' summarised Harriet. 'But my initial response is that we should involve a very specific branch of Interpol, something that we can do for you. In the meantime you should prepare a short video in the DueTube format indicating that you are willing to negotiate but need some specific information that only the kidnapper could provide. Birthmarks, that sort of thing.'

The financier nodded at the suggestions.

'One more thing,' added Caine. 'Kidnappers usually ask for much more money than they expect to get. We must offer considerably less if we are to be taken seriously.'

'Not if it endangers my sister-in-law's life,' replied Higgs.

'We'll be in touch later today,' Caine smiled as they let themselves out of the board room.

The financier, looking rather grim, waved goodbye.

Chapter 2

The journey back to their London apartment was accomplished in a driverless autotaxi, an automatically driven car which was waiting in a taxi-rank outside the HMJ-WM building. The flat was above their London office which was situated in the Caledonian Road.

'The place was very quiet for a thriving investment concern,' remarked Caine as they were driven away, noiselessly apart from a slight whirring sound from the electric motors on each of the six wheels.

'I suppose it is all done more or less automatically these days,' replied Harriet. 'They certainly don't need loads of traders or investment managers.'

'It's all in the algorithms I imagine,' agreed Caine. 'But even still it was surprisingly deserted. Why do they need such a big building if there are so few people in it?'

'It's a valuable piece of real estate,' stated Harriet. 'And it gives out the right messages to the investors. Who would want to invest in a concern that had small shabby offices?'

'I suppose that you are right,' Caine grudgingly conceded the point. 'What did you think about Benjamin Higgs?'

'Humourless,' answered Harriet. 'But then it was not a very funny situation to be in. You got him rattled when you suggested that the ransom might be ten times as large as originally imagined.'

'And even more worried when I suggested we offer considerably less,' commented Caine. 'And one thing he did not talk about was religion.'

'Should he have done?' asked Harriet.

'From the gossip I read when his wife died religion played a divisive role in their lives,' answered Caine. 'She was a Jewish lady with very unusual views whilst he was of a Christian background but had converted to Judaism when they married.'

'In what way were her views unusual?' asked Harriet as the car slowed to a halt for the nth time, stopping to let a cat cross the road.

Driverless cars were the norm now but their exact adherence to the rules of the road could be an irritation.

'She was adamant that she wanted to be cremated,' explained Caine. 'Apparently she had been proselytising the view that cremation was the sensible way forward for Judaism.'

'How did she respond to the orthodox view that burial was the only correct method?'

'She pooh poohed the attitude saying that the Mount of Olives was full and that new bodies simply displaced old ones from their resting place,' replied Caine. 'Her ashes were eventually spread on the lower slopes of the Mount of Olives despite some protests that this was against all correct procedure.'

'So why was this divisive?'

'Her family tried to insist on the immediate full burial procedure of Judaism but Higgs pointed out that he had to adhere to the views she had expressed.'

'Did the arguments become very acrimonious?'

'If I remember correctly Ben Higgs sat all night beside his dead wife in order to stop her body from being stolen. It was in all the gossip columns and blogs after one of the younger staff in the undertaker's parlour tweeted an amusing message about Higgs.'

'But do you think that this has any bearing on her sister's abduction twenty-five years ago?' Harriet was interested in the story but was not sure of its relevance

'I suppose not,' acknowledged Caine. 'But I did think he might have mentioned the controversy.'

'And this was covered in the papers?'

'Absolutely. It was all over the internet, world online, e-tabloids, etcetera,' answered Caine. 'It could have been the reason that the kidnapper got in contact.'

'Why?'

'He may have seen the coverage, realised that Maureen Higgs was Rebecca's sister and that they were fabulously wealthy.'

'Surely he knew that anyway?'

'Not necessarily,' replied Caine. 'The ransom note does rather suggest that she was taken because she was young and beautiful and he has not been trying to extort money before now.'

'Presumably she was taken for sexual reasons if she no longer amuses the kidnapper,' agreed Harriet. 'Are you assuming that the kidnapper was a man because the note was signed El Secuestrador?'

The car screeched to a halt as she asked this, the other cars behind all doing the same with the quick response of the automatic pilot. This time it was to let a fox wander aimlessly down the road.

'No,' replied Mark. 'It's just that male kidnappers are so much more common than female and would a woman have said that Rebecca no longer amuses her?'

'Perhaps,' commented Harriet. 'But unlikely.'

*

'Mum!' Charlie Caine was calling for his mother's attention. She ran over to the child who was holding a broken toy in his hands.

'It won't work, Mummy,' said the lad, poking at the toy in frustration.

'It's old, Charlie,' Harriet looked at the doll. 'This was given to me nearly thirty years ago.'

The toy was a doll that you could speak to, ask a question and it would respond after searching the internet. Mark Caine had found it in the attic and synced it to the modern net. You could once more talk to it, spell in messages, contact the net.

'You're right that the right leg is bent and the face rather battered but the doll can get through to the internet if you talk to it,' Harriet declared after examining the toy. 'I don't think that it is really broken.'

'But it's much slower than my tablet-comp and a hundred and ten times slower than the house computer interface,' replied Charlie. 'I've timed it.'

'It's just an old toy, sonny Jim,' answered Harriet tousling Charlie's hair. 'Don't worry about it.'

'I was trying to make it work better for Dad,' Charlie looked sad. 'But I can't do it.'

'It never was very fast,' explained Harriet. 'And it has limited processing capability compared with the simplest piece of modern equipment.'

'OK,' Charlie nodded his head. 'That's OK. I'll play with something else.'

*

'I've thought about it, Mr. Caine, and I don't want to inform the police,' Benjamin Higgs was talking gruffly over the screen connection.

It was early on the Tuesday morning and the financier was at home. Behind him Mark Caine could see a veritable mansion, the butler he had heard about was hovering in the background carrying a silver tray on which a glass of some kind of alcoholic beverage was poised.

'Oh there you are Jeeves,' Higgs turned round, perhaps having noticed that Caine had spotted something behind him.

Higgs took the glass from his butler and swigged the contents down in one gulp then placed the glass back on the tray. He waved the butler away with a dismissive gesture.

'Just had to take my medicine,' stated the financier.

'Oh,' Caine was surprised. 'I thought that it was something more agreeable like a glass of whisky.'

The rich investment manager's face softened and a slight smile appeared.

'You are right,' he nodded. 'It was indeed a glass of whisky. A good single malt... and I have to confess that the butler's name is not Jeeves but I always forget what it actually is and he finds the sobriquet amusing.'

'Getting back to business.....' murmured Caine.

'The police,' stated Higgs. 'I don't want them involved. It will only muddy the waters.'

'I checked up with the insurance company late yesterday and they will only honour their contract if you inform the police,' replied Caine. 'The approach can be undertaken very discreetly such that the kidnapper has no idea that you have...'

'No police,' Higgs slapped out the words, all trace of humour having vanished.

'Then our involvement must cease,' replied Caine. 'We have been employed by KNR International and they were adamant that the police must be informed such that the kidnapping is given a crime number.'

'So it's simply to keep their records straight?' queried Higgs.

'Perhaps,' agreed Caine, reluctantly. 'But kidnapping is a major crime...'

'Yeah, it's a federal crime in the USA,' interrupted Higgs. 'But this is England. Would the Gibraltar police do?'

'The Gibraltar police?'

'Yeah, why not?'

'Because the abduction originally occurred from her home in London.'

'But the ransom note came from Gibraltar according to the post mark,' the investment manager looked quizzical. 'I would be much happier if you would agree to use the police from the Rock.'

'We might, perhaps, inform the Royal Gibraltar Police,' Caine was rapidly looking up the information on his computer whilst also talking to Higgs. 'I could ask KNR if that would be acceptable but I would prefer to use the Metropolitan police.'

'If the ransom note is a hoax it emanated from Gibraltar and is a crime from that place,' replied Higgs. 'Acting on your suggestion I've put the video together and would appreciate it if the two of you could come over to my place to view it this evening.'

'At work or home?'

'Home, preferably,' replied the investment manager. 'It's in Hampstead but you don't need to dress up.'

Higgs laughed slightly as he delivered the last line. He had clearly said the same thing many times before.

*

The nanny was left to get Charlie to bed. Despite being mentally amazingly precocious Charlie needed plenty of sleep like any young child. His normal bed time was seven o'clock but tonight he was staying up till eight to watch one of his favourite programmes on the holoTV. This was a "science today" compendium, the best from three years of the show. Perhaps Charlie's absolute favourite programmes were those featuring his mother as Vanessa, the intrepid reporter for Channel 195 Live.

Harriet and Caine travelled towards Hampstead in their own auto-piloted vehicle. There was no need to take a driverless cab this time as they had been assured that there would be plenty of parking available at the Higgs' house. Hampstead was not very far at all from their place in Islington but was a world apart in its luxury.

The place was magnificent. The house looked as if it had been built in the early years of the previous century in a classical design of three stories but appearances were deceptive. The entire place had been recently rebuilt to accommodate all of the latest advances in smart technology. The butler's job was almost superfluous. The front door opened remotely, and the butler just stood to one side then led them to the large reception room where Benjamin Higgs was waiting.

Standing next to the financier were two strapping young men, identical in appearance.

'Meet Martin and Danny,' Higgs introduced the pair to the boys. 'They're my twin sons, aged twenty and very bright.'

They both looked rather embarrassed by the description but shook Harriet and Caine's hands warmly.

'I've been explaining the situation to the boys but they would like to hear it from you too,' explained Benjamin Higgs.

Harriet gave a top down description of their involvement from the point when they were first contacted by KNR and finished by saying that the kidnap and ransom firm were happy to use the Gibraltar police.

'It's a large sum of money that is involved,' added Caine. 'So they would like to bring a Gibraltar police representative over here, just to check on the validity of the claim and do a little investigation in tandem with ourselves.'

'Not too much, I hope,' countered Higgs. 'The idea that some sweaty Spanish man might be snooping around does not appeal to me.'

'The person that the Royal Gibraltar Constabulary have suggested is a very recently retired Chief Constable named Graves,' replied Harriet. 'She is highly regarded and would be very discrete.'

'A woman?' smiled Higgs, immediately mollified. 'I'm sure that would be fine. Now let's see the video.'

Higgs took the four of them over to a huge holoscreen and said the word "Play".

The screen lit up and in glorious 3D they could see Higgs sitting in the same clothes as he had been wearing the previous day. He was sat in the reception room they were presently occupying and the message was short, wasting no time in coming to the point and was entitled *25 years but now too old*, as demanded in the note.

'To whoever El Secuestrador may be. I am Benjamin Higgs,' the financier was looking earnestly at the camera. 'We will negotiate but proof that you hold the goods must be given before we will purchase. You can send messages via a quantum encrypted channel if you wish or once again by mail. My email address is available online.'

'Does that seem OK?' asked Higgs.

'I would think so,' nodded Caine. 'What do you think Harriet?'

'Fine,' agreed the investigator, wife and mother. 'I expect

that he will use the paper airmail again but you were right to suggest encryption.'

'What do you lads think?' asked Caine.

'This is our aunty we're talking about,' replied the Martin. 'And we think that she will be very much like Mum.'

'Who we miss a lot,' added Danny with a slight break in his voice.

'So we go ahead and put it up on DueTube?' asked Higgs.

Everybody nodded so he pressed a button.

'It's done,' he announced.

'Now we wait,' stated Harriet.

'Yes, now we wait,' agreed Higgs sombrely.

Chapter 3

The response came back in the post four days later. This time the butler was primed to keep the envelope, handling it with gloves on. The investigators, Harriet and Mark Caine, were at home in Bristol when they were called on the screen by the financier.

'They've upped the ante,' stated the investment manager. 'He or she is demanding more money!'

The financier held the letter up against the screen for Harriet and Mark to peruse. Higgs was handling the epistle wearing gloves.

To Higgs
She has two moles on her right buttock, half an inch apart.

From now on for every day of delay the price rises by 10%.

To prove I mean it I have put the price up to 2.2 billion pounds sterling. Let me know you will pay. Post another video on Duetube

El Secuestrador

'Is it true about the moles?' asked Harriet.

'I think it might be,' Higgs looked perturbed. 'The only person I can think to ask is her old nanny, Miss Amelia Stevenson.'

'She's still alive?'

'She is,' Higgs replied in the affirmative. 'She's in her eighties and lives in sheltered accommodation.'

'Is she likely to remember?' asked Mark Caine.

'Oh, I expect so,' replied the financier. 'She hasn't lost any of her intelligence. Mind you she had moved on to another family way before Rebecca disappeared so she is not likely to know any more about that.'

'It would still be worth asking when we ask about the moles,' suggested Harriet.

'Of course, if you wish,' agreed Higgs. 'She is rather conveniently situated for you two.'

'Where does she live?' asked Mark.

'She retired to Weston-super-Mare and is now in a residential home there,' replied the financier.

*

'Oh yes,' warbled the old lady, sat in her favourite rocking chair in the communal sitting room, her sheitel firmly attached to her head . 'She certainly did have two moles on her right buttock. Quite large ones though they may have seemed smaller when she was older.'

Harriet had driven over to Weston the next day, Sunday, as

it was only a short distance from their home in Bristol. It was clear that the nanny had lost none of her brightness, her eyes burned with intelligence but her body was weak.

'Were you around when she disappeared?' asked Harriet.

'Oh no, dear,' answered the old nanny. 'I had left the Cohen's employment long before then.'

'What was Rebecca like?'

'She was always the wild one,' replied the old dear. 'So I was not surprised when she left. I assumed that she had gone because she could not stand the stifling nature of the family.'

'Stifling?'

'They were ultra-orthodox,' the nanny sighed. 'So many people revolt against over-excessive religious practice.'

'Yes,' agreed Harriet. 'I suppose they do.'

'So I assumed that she had left of her own free will. It's a shock to hear that she was abducted. If we had ever really suspected that we might have worked harder to find her.'

'You talk as if you felt as if you were still involved with the family,' remarked Harriet.

'But I was, dear,' answered the nanny. 'I became a family friend and would see them fairly often at the various festivals, Passover, Hanukah, Bat Mitzvah.'

'And what of Maureen Cohen?' Harriet inquired.

'She was a surprise,' the nanny nodded her head. 'Definitely a surprise.'

'In what way?'

'She married out. He did convert but he was not of Jewish descent.'

'Did the family object?'

'At first but since they had lost the other girl they felt obliged to be more accommodating than they had previously been.'

'Did they become reconciled to the marriage?'

'Completely, though they struggled with Maureen's unconventional views on cremation versus burial. Who would have thought that Maureen would die so soon after her parents?'

'I understand she had a long illness?' suggested Harriet.

'Something like MS or ME I think,' replied the old nanny. 'Though the diagnosis was always rather vague, if I recall correctly.'

Which I am certain that you do, thought the female investigator. She could not stop herself from having another stare at the old lady's wig, or sheitel. It was certainly an unusual sight and competed with the view of the pier, once again rebuilt after an arson attack had destroyed a lot of it.

*

'The forensic scientists have not found very much on the ransom notes or the envelope,' Harriet was speaking to Benjamin Higgs over the screens from their office on London.

'What have they found?' asked the financier, anxious to learn the news.

'Very common paper and envelope,' stated Harriet. 'The only fingerprints are yours and the butlers on the first note. None at all on the second or the envelope. Traces of DNA ... yours and the butler's on all three, several presently unknown on the envelope but only yours on the interior of the second note.'

'Anything else? No traces of Rebecca's?' asked the financier. 'If they really do have her it is possible that they may have shown her the note,crowing or whatever.'

'Good point,' answered Harriet. 'She could be one of the unknown traces but we don't have a sample of Rebecca's DNA.'

'Would it be the same as Maureen's?' asked Higgs.

'If they truly were identical then the answer presumably is yes,' replied Harriet.

'I can send you a lock of Maureen's hair, taken when she was very young,' suggested the financier. 'Would that help?'

'It would be of enormous assistance,' agreed Harriet. 'But don't send it. I shall be right over and fetch it myself. I'll probably be at your house in about forty-five minutes, if that's OK.'

'Totally fine.'

*

'She had long dark hair but cut it short after breaking up with her first boyfriend aged just thirteen,' explained Ben Higgs to Harriet when she arrived at the house.

'So this is a lock of Maureen's hair from that time?' concluded Harriet, looking at a locket containing a photograph and a lock of still dark, lustrous hair.

'That's right,' agreed Higgs. 'Will that do for the analysis?'

'It's not as easy to extract DNA from hair as it is from an inner cheek sample,' replied Harriet. 'But since a buccal sample is impossible it should be sufficient.'

*

'The answer is that the unknown DNA does not match Maureen's,' Harriet was talking over the screen. 'Of course it could be from any random person who had been near the paper.'

'So there is no proof that Rebecca is alive,' stated Higgs.

'Nor does it prove she is dead,' countered Harriet.

'I am inclined to forego the pleasure of handing over 2.2 billion pounds on the evidence of a couple of moles that the kidnapper might have seen twenty-five years ago,' muttered the hard-nosed businessman.

'Have you had a further demand?'

'None,' replied Higgs. 'Let's hope that it stays that way.'

'Have you posted another video?'

'No,' answered Higgs. 'And I don't intend doing so.'

*

'A terrible thing has happened,' screamed Higgs over the screen.

It was Saturday. Caine and Harriet were at home in Bristol.

'What terrible thing?' asked Caine.

'El Secuestrador has sent me an ear in the post,' stated Higgs. 'I will have to pay up or he will kill her.'

'You are sure it is Rebecca's ear?'

'You can test it for DNA but it looks very much like my wife's ear so I suspect it really is Rebecca's.'

'How did it come to you?' Caine was intrigued.

'In a thermos packed with ice,' replied Higgs. 'It's been cleaned up, there's very little blood on it but it is indubitably a female human ear and almost certainly Rebecca's.'

'I will have to travel up to London on the fast train,' Mark was resigned to his weekend being ruined. The time in Malaga was fast fading in his mind.

*

'The ear has been tested for DNA and it is definitely the same as Maureen's as far as they can tell from the hair sample,' stated Harriet over the screen.

'So it is her twin Rebecca's ear?' sighed Higgs. 'I was hoping that it wasn't.'

'That is the assumption we are working on,' agreed Harriet. 'The police representative would like to meet you today. She has been looking into all of this quietly in the background.'

'Certainly,' the financier assented. 'We should all meet. We need to get the transfer of funds sorted out as soon as possible.'

'I've spoken to KNR International,' stated Harriet. 'They are prepared to proceed with the transfer of funds as long as you are happy for the results to be made public if the return of Rebecca is successful.'

'We've been liquidating assets,' replied Higgs. 'But we do need the part that the insurance covers in order to make up the full amount. Given more time I could have made up the total from our own funds but the sale of shares has proceeded.'

'OK,' nodded Harriet. 'I understand. Do you have an address to send the funds to?'

'I've received another note with all the bank account details for the electronic transfer of funds to the kidnapper,' answered Higgs.

'We will need to analyse that as well,' demanded Harriet.

'You can do that but I doubt that it will do much good,' sighed Higgs.

Chapter 4

'Hello,' said the slim attractive but grey-haired lady, holding out her hand. 'At last we meet. I'm Penelope Graves.'

The Caines, Benjamin Higgs and Penelope Graves were meeting in the board room of Higgs' company. Benjamin shook the retired police woman's proffered hand.

'I have been available all along,' stated the financier. 'I'm not trying to hide from you.'

'I've been busy behind the scenes,' Graves spoke quietly but with an air of authority. 'The Caines have been very helpful.'

'Where have you got so far?' asked Higgs.

'I've checked up on the various post offices on the Rock,' stated Graves. 'Not much snail mail goes through there these days apart from holiday postcards.'

'Oh!' the financier was surprised.

'So it was fairly easy to discover that this was sent from an automated postal drop box.'

'What does that mean?' asked Higgs.

'Someone could send the letter in a covering envelope. The machine discards the outer cover, reads the address on the inner envelope and sends it on,' stated Graves. 'It is all done automatically.'

'So the kidnapper does not necessarily live on the Rock of Gibraltar?' queried Higgs.

'It is highly unlikely that he or she lives anywhere near Gibraltar,' pronounced Graves.

'So we are no further on and the fund transfer must continue?' suggested the financier.

'We will see what we can do with future letters but the answer so far is in the affirmative.'

'I will have to respond extremely soon now that he has started mutilating Rebecca,' Higgs looked depressed.

'Yes,' agreed Graves. 'Are we all in agreement that the funds should be transferred?'

The Caines and Higgs nodded their approval of the transfer and Higgs pressed a button on his computer.

'A very simple task pressing a small button but that action transferred one and a half billion pounds from my account.'

'And five hundred million from KNR International,' stated Mark Caine.

'Followed by an interrogative spike from the insurance company,' remarked Harriet.

'What?' screamed Benjamin Higgs, 'That could endanger Rebecca's life!'

'And yours,' declared Penelope Graves. 'I am arresting you, Benjamin Higgs, for fraudulently obtaining five hundred million pounds from KNR International insurance company and illegally transferring money from Martin and Daniel's accounts.'

'That was done with their full cooperation,' shouted the financier. 'Graves, you are way out of line and you have no powers of arrest. Caine, I shall see you in hell for this!'

'I doubt it,' countered Graves. 'Firstly I still have my powers of arrest through special arrangement with the Met police. Secondly we have evidence that the ear was not from Rebecca Cohen.'

'But you told me that it was?' Higgs stared at Harriet.

'I told you that it was our working hypothesis,' argued Harriet. 'And now we have changed that hypothesis.'

'This is completely mad!'

The rich investment manager looked round wildly and tried to make a break for the door just as Graves phone rang.

'Right I see,' she said into the old-fashioned mobile. 'I understand.'

She looked up at the surprised faces of Harriet and Mark.

'Don't worry,' she remarked. 'He won't get far. I've placed officers outside and they'll catch him immediately.'

*

Ten minutes later they were sat in the board room and two burly male detectives returned with Higgs in toe.

'Good,' commented Graves. 'To that short list of crimes I am adding a couple more. Mutilating a corpse by cutting off the ear and murder most foul. Poisoning of your wife over a long period of time using Thallium or a similar heavy metal poison. I must caution you that anything you say may be taken down as evidence and used against you...'

'Rubbish,' screeched the financier. 'Let me go. I'm a billionaire. You can't handle me like this.'

'If you don't shut up they will sit on you,' Graves spoke quietly but with determination and the financier calmed down considerably.

'I shall continue,' stated the policewoman. 'You have a right to remain silent and a right to have a solicitor. Anything you say may be taken down and used in evidence against you.'

Graves phone rang again.

'Right,' she spoke into it more loudly than was strictly necessary. 'So it definitely was Thallium, the poisoner's poison.'

'Where did you find Thallium?' asked Higgs. 'Was it in the ear?'

'It was indeed in the ear,' stated Graves. 'The ear of your wife.'

'No, no,' Higgs shook his head. 'Rebecca's ear, Rebecca's ear.'

'I'm afraid not,' replied Graves. 'You see, identical twins have very similar DNA, almost identical, but not quite so. There are small differences in the epigenetic changes and even in the DNA of the genes.'

'How can that be?' questioned the financier. 'I don't think that you can prove anything. You haven't got any DNA that you know is from Rebecca.'

'We have had the help of your sons,' replied Graves. 'And they are definitely your wife's children. Their DNA is compatible with the the ear and there are slight changes that have accumulated since the hair was obtained.'

'So?' Higgs looked confused. 'You'd expect my sons DNA to

match my wife's.'

'But they do not match your DNA.'

'My DNA?'

'Yes, you gave the Caines a sample when they were analysing the note,' answered Graves. 'The boys are not your sons and I reckon you knew that.'

Higgs expression became more resigned.

'And you decided to murder your wife and remove her ear.'

'Why would I do that and then concoct all of this farrago?' asked the financier.

'Because the money was effectively entailed,' replied Graves. 'Harriet and Mark have done a very good job analysing the shares of your company and the vast majority belong to the boys, not to you.'

'This is absurd.'

'Absurd but true,' replied Graves. 'The murder was unsuspected by the police and would have been a perfect crime if you had not been greedy and wanted all of the money for yourself, perhaps as punishment to the lads for not actually being your sons?'

'Don't talk rubbish!'

'The sheitel covered two problems at her funeral... she was almost hairless due to the Thallium poisoning and only had one ear. No wonder you wanted her to be cremated.'

'It's just not true!'

'I'm sorry but it is. The only loose end to the story was what had really happened to Rebecca? Was she complicit in the crime?'

'She is the victim of a kidnapper twenty-five years ago....' the financier's voice tailed off as he looked at the policewoman. Graves was completely ignoring the bluster.

'But that was solved by a worldwide advertisement,' the police woman added. 'Rebecca Cohen contacted us yesterday.'

'But she's dead!'

'No she isn't,' countered Graves. 'She is alive and well and living in Argentina.'

Graves looked at her antique watch, a timepiece that required winding.

'In fact right now she is on a shuttle coming here. I took the liberty of telling her about your imminent arrest and she has decided to return to meet her nephews. At least they will have one relative who will love them.'

'Love them?' screamed Higgs. 'You don't know them and nor does she. They are spawn of the devil and they don't deserve my money.'

With frantic strength the financier broke free from the two police who were holding him and ran for the window. He hurled himself at the plate glass, expecting it to break, and then lay back stunned.

'It's not so easy to throw yourself out of a multistory office block now that they are hermetically sealed passive buildings with triple-glazed unbreakable windows,' remarked Mark.

'And we're only on the ground floor anyway,' stated Harriet, with a grin.

*

'I have some interesting news,' stated Penny Graves over the huge flat screen in the front office of Caine's London address.

'Go ahead,' replied Mark.

'The two of you were worried about the lack of activity in Higgs' HQ, right?'

'We were,' agreed Mark. 'For a massive financial concern the place was eerily calm.'

'We've discovered the reason,' reported Graves. 'One area was sealed off and we forced entry.'

'What was in there?' asked Mark, intrigued.

'You'll be interested in this,' returned Penny. 'A Holmberg Effect machine.'

'A time machine? Where did they get that from, they're strictly experimental.'

'Seems not,' countered Penny Graves. 'Apparently Benjamin Higgs has been using it to predict the future of stocks and shares.'

'So he literally bought futures?' commented Mark. 'But how did he overcome the problem of size? The largest object they could get through the machine was a bottle of wine!'

'I've no idea but he did it somehow, hence the massive growth in the company,' Penny looked away, obviously interrupted. 'They're trying to get hold of me for something. I'll be right back.'

Her face disappeared from the screen but the police station she was standing in was still displayed. Suddenly from the next room in the small Islington office Harriet gave a scream. She came running into the front office obviously in a panic. Simultaneously a very perturbed Penny appeared back on the screen and started speaking.

'Stop, stop,' cried Mark. 'I can't listen to both of you at once.'

'Let Harriet speak first,' suggested Penny, her professional calm returning.

'Someone has kidnapped Charlie and assaulted the nanny,' cried Harriet breathlessly. 'She had just taken Charlie into our hallway in Bristol, I think they were going out, when a man knocked on the front door. She opened it and the man hit her in the face, knocking her over. He grabbed Charlie and scooped him into a car and drove off.'

'What was the description?' asked Graves

'Man in his forties, not much else,' replied Harriet. 'She didn't manage to take down the number plate as she was still stunned from being knocked down.'

'I think that my news might tie in with that,' suggested Penny Graves.

'How?' asked Mark.

'Some incompetent fools have let Benjamin Higgs escape.'

'When?' shouted Mark.

'How?' shouted Harriet.

'About two hours ago which just about gives him time to have driven to Bristol,' answered Graves. 'And he escaped by climbing out through a lavatory window. The oldest trick in the book.'

'So you think he might have taken my little boy?' queried Harriet, holding back a sob.

'It's a major possibility,' replied Graves. 'They've put an all out alert for Higgs cars and any sighting of the man.'

'Wait,' said Harriet. 'There's a strange text coming through to my mobile. It's from that old toy doll that you mended for Charlie.'

BENJAMIN HAS GOT ME. HE IS NOT A NICE MAN. HE MADE ME LEEF MY FONE BUT I TOOK THE DOLL. ITS SLOW. I WOTCHED WEN WE WERE DRIVING. THE HOUSE IS IN LOVE LANE, BURNHAM ON SEA. NUMBER 5. BENJAMIN HAS GONE OUT

'How old did you say that boy is?' asked Graves.

'Three,' replied Harriet.

'Three?' Graves was astounded. 'He writes like an adult.'

'He's precocious,' agreed Harriet. 'But he really is only a very little boy. We will have to do something about his spelling.'

Graves still looked completely astonished.

'And you haven't chipped his brain?'

'No need,' replied Mark.

'Well we had better organise a rescue party,' Penelope Graves was speaking into her mobile as well as talking over the screen. 'That's done. A party of plain clothes detectives from the Burnham police station will go to the house, collect little Charlie and then wait for Benjamin Higgs to return.'

'What if he gets there before they do?' asked Harriet, still in a panic.

'I reckon that boy can sort out Higgs,' replied Graves. 'But don't worry. They are on their way right now. In the meantime I shall pop round to your office.'

*

Penelope Graves had travelled the relatively short distance to the Caine's office by the time she heard back from the Burnham police. The face of the local sergeant appeared on the large screen.

'We've got little Charlie and Benjamin Higgs,' said the sergeant. 'A young lady is coming to fetch Charlie, is that right?'

'Her name?' asked Graves.

'Susan Sidebottom,' replied the uniformed policeman.

Penelope Graves looked questioningly at Harriet and Mark. They nodded their agreement.

'That's fine,' Graves replied to Burnham. 'Be careful with Higgs. He has escaped twice.'

'We've handcuffed him and locked him in a cell.'

'Fine.'

*

'It turns out that Higgs had a very simple way of interrogating the future,' stated Graves, back in the Caine's office two days later.

'What was that?' asked Mark. 'You couldn't personally travel there using the chrono-spatial displacement technique of Professor Holmberg.'

'He didn't try to. He used a litter picker.'

'A litter picker? What good would that do?' asked Mark

'You don't need to go into the future yourself to find out what is going to happen,' explained Penny Graves. 'What Higgs did was to regularly leave a printout of the day's financial listings in a set place next to the outlet of the machine. As long as this was done every day it was possible to poke the litter pickers through the machine and pick the pages from days in the future. He could then read off the results and predict which shares were the best bet, which currency to buy or sell, which futures to hold. It was dead easy.'

'So Karl Raven could have done the same?' surmised Harriet.

'Of course,' agreed Graves. 'But he did not think of it.'

'With such an advantage why did Higgs stop making money that way and turn to crime?' asked Mark.

'Because he found that after a certain period he stopped being able to collect the information. He was no longer placing the printouts in position.'

'And that made him turn to crime?' Mark was amazed.

'Yes,' replied Graves. 'Since he did it regularly every day he reckoned that he must either be dead or somebody or something was preventing him from putting the printout in position.'

'We know now what that is,' suggested Harriet.

'We do indeed,' smiled Graves. 'It's because he is locked up in jail.'

'But if he hadn't turned to crime he wouldn't be locked up,' protested Mark. 'His knowledge of the future only harmed him in the end.'

'Such is the irony,' concluded Graves.

NOTE

The policewoman Penelope Graves, at an earlier age, featured prominently in my thriller series available as ebooks. The books in the trilogy are entitled *The Confessions of Saul, The Writing on the Wall* and *Reincarnation*.

I have recently penned a further novel in which Penny Graves and her team have star roles and this is called *The Fellowship of the Egg*.

Next we have a short story about characters who appeared in my novel Oberon's Bane. The main characters are a leprechaun and a lady from the seventeenth century who now lives in the twenty-first century. This is definitely fantasy but the leprechaun has the useful ability to move in time using a magic flute, very befitting in an anthology of past, present and future short stories.

The Great Khan

The rapping at the door would not stop so Jane finally decided she would have to answer it. She reluctantly put down the book she was reading and stood up.

Jane was still marvelling about the quality of printing on modern 21st century books compared with her own time, the era of the restoration of the monarchy in 1660. It was best not to get her onto the subject of computers and the internet or robots and driverless cars.

Standing on the threshold was Randulph, the time travelling leprechaun, looking much like a magnified garden ornament.

'Quick,' he stated, pulling out a small, black wooden flute. 'Stand right there on the portal. We must go and investigate '

'However shall we do that?' asked Jane, bemused.

'Resonating thaumaturgy,' replied the little mage. 'Magic!'

'Resonating with what?' asked Jane.

The little man pulled out a coin from his pocket and Jane peered at it closely.

'Is that an elephant?' she asked, pointing at the tiny blurred image on the small copper coin.

'It is,' replied the leprechaun, smugly. 'With someone riding on it.'

'But why are we investigating an elephant?' asked the former courtier of Charles II.

'Genghis Khan,' answered the mage. 'That's why.'

'That's a who, not a why,' countered Jane.

'That's who we are off to see using this coin as a homing device,' laughed the leprechaun.

'But why?' asked the former friend of the restored Stuart monarch. 'He's a violent dictator. Surely he's a man to avoid?'

'Research on DNA has previously shown that one in every two hundred persons is descended from the fellow but our recent study has shown alarming variations from this.'

'Alarming?'

'One in every three Devonians descended from Genghis Khan is alarming, don't you think?'

'That's not possible. A third of Devon's inhabitants descended from him?' queried Jane. 'There was no obvious Oriental input when I was there in 1660.'

'That's what makes it so strange because there is now....and from studies of disinterred bones it goes back at least two centuries. And the count is rising.'

'It would have to go back a lot further than that,' countered Jane. 'Genghis Khan died in about 1227.'

'Yes, having conquered 12 million square miles of territory.'

'But he never got over here, did he?'

'No, he didn't cross the Danube.'

'So how could one in three be descended from him?'

'And rising! Now that's the mystery. Perhaps our history is wrong or is being changed?'

'So we investigate?'

'We do. Let's go.'

'Wait!' protested Jane. 'David would probably like to come

with us.'

'Is he at home?' asked the little mage.

'Not right now but he'll be back soon.'

'Can't wait,' muttered the leprechaun blowing his flute. 'Must go now.'

Jane felt the usual sensation of icy chill flow over her body as the ethereal modal notes cut through the air and through time itself. In touch with the music of the spheres the ancient time magic worked its charms and the portal of the flat faded away to be replaced by rolling hills and a burbling river. Off in the distance beyond the heather moorland a rugged coastline could be seen.

'I expected to end up in Mongolia,' remarked the little mage. 'This is certainly not a landlocked country in Asia.'

'No it isn't,' replied Jane crossly. 'That's the Vale of Porlock. I know exactly where we are. We're on Exmoor.'

'Presumably back in the thirteenth century,' stated Randulph.

'Maybe and maybe not,' countered Jane. 'Those houses in the distance don't look thirteenth century. They look much newer in style.'

'I suppose you're right,' answered Randulph grudgingly.

'Of course I am,' replied Jane. 'They were not even here when I knew the place in the seventeenth century.'

They stood arguing for a few more moments and were unaware of the presence of a horde of horsemen who had quietly ridden up behind them.

'Seize the girl,' cried the leader of the riding men. 'And kill the little dwarf.'

'Wait, wait, wait,' cried Randulph, dancing nimbly out of the way of the swordsmen on horseback. 'Take me with you too. I can be very useful.'

The swordsmen kept missing the agile leprechaun and eventually the leader signalled to his men to stop trying to kill Randulph.

'Will you surrender if I agree not to kill you?' asked the chief horseman.

'Yes,' said Randulph, holding up a clean white handkerchief.

'Bind him tightly,' nodded the leader. 'We shall take him to the Great Khan.'

Jane and Randulph were tied to the backs of spare horses and the posse set off. After what felt like an age of painful galloping bumps but really was only a few minutes they rounded a hill and could look down into a valley. It was an amazing sight ….. giant tents … a huge camp and one enormous domed yurt in the middle.

Guards were lined around the perimeter.

'We will take you to the mighty Khan,' stated the leader as he pulled the group to a halt.

'Genghis, the great Khan?' queried Randulph

'Not Genghis,' contradicted the horseman. 'Kubla Khan!'

The riders had all dismounted and they now untied their captives and hastened them along towards the giant tent.

Sat on a huge throne,surrounded by dancing girls, belly dancers, pipers, snake charmers and courtiers was Kubla Khan himself. Standing in one corner, huddled in a group, were a few local Devon people heavily guarded by the Khan's wild-eyed soldiers.

'What have you and this slip of a girl done to my paradise, my Xanadu?' asked the Khan aggressively when the pair were thrust in front of him.

'Why do you think we had anything to do with it?' asked

Jane.

'One moment we are in the middle of my empire and the next we are here. You are on site so who else should I blame?'

'What about the other people you have captured?' demanded Jane feistily.

'They know nothing and they do not have the stance of bold leaders that you do,' replied the Khan. 'And they cannot speak in Mongolian.'

'Oh, that's fascinating, ' grinned the leprechaun. 'Xanadu! And my magic is translating our speech perfectly.'

'And it's sometime around 1797,' stated Jane, stooping to the ground and lifting up an object. 'I've found a huge copper coin with the date on it.'

She held up the coin an Randulph stared at it.

'A cartwheel tuppence in perfect condition,' mused the mage. 'We're in North Devon, on or abouts 1797. That date rings a bell... and, of course, Xanadu. Now what do they remind me of?"

'It should ring a bell,' agreed Jane. 'I've just been reading about it.'

'About what?'

'Samuel Taylor Coleridge,' replied Jane. 'The poet. I've just been reading an anthology of his poems.'

'Go on....'

'Fine,' agreed Jane. 'Here's the first verse.

'In Xanadu did Kubla Khan
A stately pleasure-dome decree:
Where Alph, the sacred river, ran
Through caverns measureless to man
Down to a sunless sea.'

'Yes,' cried the great Khan, leaping down from his throne, who had been listening intently to the conversation. 'That is the verse that keeps going through my head. And where are we? What are these hills and what is this sea?'

'This is Devon,' replied Jane.

'Are you demon lovers?' asked the great Khan, staring wildly at the dwarf and the girl.

'No, no,no ... but somehow you have been transported to Devon from Mongolia,' Jane said quickly, before the usual treatment for demons was meted out.

'And I might just know how,' added the leprechaun. 'Or at least, I may have an inkling of why.'

The Khan, the fabled leader of the Horde and grandson of Genghis, stared at the little man.

'Jane has prompted my memory,' continued Randulph. 'It's not exactly the same, you know, but it might just work if you can take us to Lynmouth.'

'You are going nowhere,' the great Khan signalled to his men. 'Lock them up. We will execute them later.'

The time travelling leprechaun and Jane, the Seventeenth century society IT girl, were taken to a different tent with furry leather walls, a wooden door and a primitive lock.

Randulph sat down on a cushion and started to reminisce.

'Did I ever tell you that I was the person who gave the Mongols the idea of using silk underwear when they went into battle?'

'It's not the right time to tell me now,' groaned Jane. 'This surely wasn't what you planned when you dragged me along. Or was it?'

'More or less,' admitted the little leprechaun.

'That we would be tied up, bundled onto a horse and thrown into a locked, smelly leather tent!' exclaimed Jane. 'You're beyond reckless, Randulph!'

'But at least we know now what is going on.'

'We do?'

'Of course we do,' replied the leprechaun. 'More resonating thaumaturgy. The musical magic of the spheres....'

'By Samuel....?'

'.....Taylor Coleridge himself,' Randulph finished Jane's sentence.

The leprechaun freed himself from the slack ropes that they had been rebound in before being thrust into the leather tent. He bounced over to the lock, touched it and blew a few notes on his flute. The primitive lock clicked open and the leprechaun peered out.

'It's all clear, follow me.'

Obeying the little leprechaun Jane tiptoed out of the tent and over to a pair of horses. The leprechaun stood starring at the beasts.

'Help me up,' ordered the little man.

Jane looked at him in surprise.

'They're too big for me to climb onto,' explained the leprechaun in a hissing whisper. 'So help me up!'

Jane picked up the tiny mage and put him on the horse.

'Now get on behind me!' demanded Randulph.

With a shrug of her shoulders Jane obeyed the command.

'It's a relatively small horse,' she muttered as she sat astride the ornate cloth saddle.

'It's still huge to me,' replied the leprechaun through gritted teeth.

'I get the impression that you don't like horses,' laughed Jane.

'They're OK,' replied the mage. 'At the front of a cart or in dog meat.'

The horse whinnied and bucked at this.

'Ooops,' cried the leprechaun. 'I forgot that the magic could translate my words into horse speech. Nice horsey, that's a nice horsey!'

The pony calmed down but the damage had been done. Warriors poked their heads out of the surrounding tents and grabbed for their spears and swords.

Jane and Randulph rode out of the camp followed, at a distance, by hordes of angry Mongolians.

Around the hill and out of site from the following horsemen, the leprechaun pulled abruptly on the reins, directing the small horse into a wooded copse.

'We'll wait for the posse to pass,' explained the leprechaun. 'Then ride back in the opposite direction.'

'I was going to tell you that Lynmouth is in that direction,' stated Jane pointing. 'And not the way we were going.'

The horde passed by with much hooting and hollering and when they had disappeared Randulph turned the horse round and they rode off along the coastal path.

Part way along their route Jane and Randulph could see

strange lights in the sky flickering in multi-coloured hues above a very small church.

'That's Culbone Church,' pronounced Jane. 'It's the smallest church in England.'

'I don't think he is actually in the church,' remarked the mage. 'The flickering seems to emanate from that small cottage.'

They rode towards the house past a sign saying 'Ash Farm.' Tying the pony to a post they entered a simple abode that had turned into an other-worldly place.

Inside Samuel Taylor Coleridge was in a trance, chanting words continually.

> *'A savage place! as holy and enchanted*
> *As e'er beneath a waning moon was haunted*
> *By woman wailing for her demon-lover!'*

In front of Coleridge was a hazy image of Kubla Khan, still sitting on his silk cushions in the large tent. He was receiving a deputation from his warriors and then sending them out again.

'That's not actually a demon,' corrected Randulph. 'Strictly speaking that is a trans-temporal manifestation of Kubla Khan captured by the amazing resonance of Coleridge's voice and the astonishing evocation of imagery in his words.'

'His voice has brought Kubla Khan through time to Porlock?' Jane was astonished. 'It's amazing enough that we can move through space and time using the music of your pipe but how can Coleridge's voice capture Kubla Khan and his entourage?'

'In just the same way that the pipe works,' replied the leprechaun. 'It is the music of the spheres. I expect that Coleridge has an object he is focussing on that was from the time of the great Khans.'

They stood silently and watched the diorama as Coleridge continued to chant

'It flung up momently the sacred river.
Five miles meandering with a mazy motion
Through wood and dale the sacred river ran,
Then reached the caverns measureless to man,
And sank in tumult to a lifeless ocean'

Bang, CRASH!

The following horsemen, realising their mistake, had turned round and followed the trail of the pony. The armed soldiers were now banging at the door of the cottage. Jane peeked out of the window and could see dozens of Kubla Khan's followers.

'We're surrounded,' she gasped.

'I thought as much,' muttered Randulph. 'I'm afraid we will have to stop the manifestation.'

The little leprechaun ran forward and shook Samuel Taylor Coleridge sharply. The poet continued to chant, his eyes glazed, the pupils pinpoint.

'That sunny dome! Those caves of ice!
And all who heard should see them there,
And all should cry, Beware! Beware!
His flashing eyes, his floating hair!
Weave a circle round him thrice,
And close your eyes with holy dread
For he on honey-dew hath fed,
And drunk the milk of Paradise.'

'The integrity of the timeline has to be insured,' stated Randulph, shaking Coleridge even more sharply.

'Not to mention the integrity of the local girls,' added Jane.

Samuel Taylor Coleridge was waking from his drug-induced

trance and looking round at his surroundings, his eyes wild. As he did so the image of the Great Khan gradually faded and the clamour at the door of the small house died away.

Jane looked out again. The lane was clear.

The poet was now fully awake.

'I heard you talk about Porlock and now you talk about Insurance. You must go, I have no interest in Insurance or any such thing. Just go.'

Coleridge had taken up a quill pen and was starting to scratch the poem down upon a piece of linen paper.'

'No, no, we are not here about insurance, we are simple travelers,' Randulph tried to put the record straight but the poet was not listening. He was scribbling as fast as he was able.

After fifteen minutes of the hectic scribbling he looked up and saw Randulph and Jane watching him.

'Are you still here?' he asked. 'I told you to go so why haven't you left? You insurance men are all the same.'

'I'm not an insurance man from Porlock,' cried the leprechaun, jumping up and down in rage. 'Do I look like an insurance man? I'm not even in a suit, I'm tiny. I'm a wrinkled leprechaun for the love of mercy. A leprechaun!'

Samuel Taylor Coleridge rubbed his eyes.

'That Laudanum is making me see the weirdest visions today. First the Kubla Khan at Xanadu and now an insurance man who has shrunk to the size of a leprechaun.'

He continued to rub his eyes and shake his head.

'I must have taken more than I thought and now this accursed man from Porlock is messing me up even more. I can only remember a few lines of my poem and a general description of Xanadu. I must have composed several hundred lines and now...just a few remain.'

The poet struggled to write a few more verses then looked up once more.

'Get out Porlock man!' he screamed in rage when he saw Randulph again.

'I think it really is time we left,' agreed Jane, pulling Randulph towards the door. 'But how did his magic work?'

'As I said. The music of the spheres.'

'Which is?'

'Quantum telepathy via entangled pairs which does not recognize the barrier of distance or even time,' mused Randulph as he was dragged away by the society girl. 'I disturbed his flow and unfortunately he won't remember the rest of the lines.'

'He'll remember the man from Porlock,' remarked Jane.

'But not the woman, strangely enough,' came the rejoinder.

NOTE

Coleridge has long been my favourite poet and I was delighted to meet one of his descendants, a Dr Simon Taylor-Coleridge, who was working at the Bristol Royal Infirmary. We spent a happy time discussing the great man and his work. If you have not read any of Coleridge's work then *Kubla Khan* is a good place to start but the *Rime of the Ancient Mariner* is my favourite.

> *Water, water, every where,*
> *And all the boards did shrink;*
> *Water, water, every where,*
> *Nor any drop to drink.*

We remain in the fantasy world of Randulph the leprechaun for the next story. An anthology of fantasy and science fiction would not be complete without a few frightening aliens.

The image of the Pavilion is courtesy of "Svencb" via Wikipedia.

Brighton Pavilion

'Quickly,' ordered the tiny mage otherwise known as Randulph the leprechaun.

'What is it this time?' asked Jane, having only just recovered from her jaunt to 1797 and her tussles with the anachronistic Mongol hordes.

'Where's David?' asked the tiny breathless figure. 'There's no time to waste!'

'There never is with you,' sighed Jane. 'Why don't you come in and have a nice cup of tea, calm down a little and take it easy.'

'This is an emergency!'

'When was it ever different?' asked Jane with a wry smile. 'The kettle is already boiling so it won't take a moment to pop a tea bag into the pot.'

'Oh OK,' agreed Randulph reluctantly. 'But we will need to get a move on.'

The leprechaun took his sprightly figure into the front hall, looking at the various mementoes on the wall as he did so. An oil painting of a very happy cavalier, given by King Charles the Second to Jane, dominated the scene. Jane smiled when she saw where Randulph's eyes had alighted.

'That picture always makes me feel happy and takes me back to my home century,' she remarked.

They moved into the kitchen and Randulph was relieved to see that the kettle was indeed on the boil.

'But where is David?' asked the tiny mage, glancing around as if his time travelling partner would pop out of a drawer at any moment.

'He's away again and this time he won't be back until tomorrow evening,' answered Jane as she poured out two cups of Lady Grey. 'How do you like it?'

'Like it?' cried Randulph. 'I don't like it. I need him right now. I need David's help!'

'I meant the tea,' sighed Jane. 'I've managed to adapt to the modern world, Randulph, so why don't you?'

'It's easier to adapt when you are from the past,' muttered the leprechaun. 'I'm from a long way in the future. That is much harder.'

'Why?' asked Jane, intrigued despite her deep felt misgivings and forebodings that she was about to get into another adventure with the little mage, an adventure that could go terribly wrong, The explanation might just be the start of that adventure.

'It's to do with the laws of thermodynamics,' explained the mage. 'You've moved with the arrow of time whilst I've moved against it.'

'But what I really wanted to know was whether you desired milk and sugar with your tea or liked it plain?'

'Doesn't everybody have their tea just with water?' asked the mage. 'It would be weird to have it with milk and I have to warn you that there are health hazards of taking too much sugar.'

'So you'd like it plain?'

'No,' stated the leprechaun, perversely. 'I think I will try it with milk and three sugars. Why not?'

Jane decided not to argue. It was never wise to argue with a time travelling leprechaun from the future especially when it was being capricious. When they had finished the rather pleasant cup of tea the leprechaun stood up.

'If David is not returning you will have to come with me, right now.'

'Where are we going?' sighed Jane. 'And how should I dress?'

'Early Nineteenth century is the period and Brighton is the place,' exclaimed the tiny mage. 'And if you have any demon-proof garments they might help.'

'Demon-proof?' queried Jane. 'Are there such clothes?'

'I don't know,' answered Randulph. 'But we are about to find out.'

*

'Why are we travelling by public transport when we could use your magic flute?' asked Jane as the train pulled out of the station, moving south.

'The less interference the better,' replied the mage mysteriously.

'But surely you intend interfering and that is why you have dragged me along,' protested the former courtier of Charles the Second.

'I do, indeed, but only in the correct century and in the right place,' sighed the leprechaun. 'I've learnt my lesson. From now on less is more.'

Jane was baffled.

'Then why interfere at all?'

'This time we have to,' remarked Randulph. 'Duty calls!'

From Brighton railway station Randulph led Jane at a brisk walk towards the Royal Pavilion.

'I've read about the Pavilion,' said Jane, breathlessly as she tried to keep up with the surprisingly quick leprechaun. 'But I've never seen it. It did not exist in my century.'

'Of course it didn't,' muttered the little mage, a bit abruptly. 'It was built between 1787 and 1823.'

'For the Prince Regent who was later George IV,' added Jane. 'Yes, I know that. But why are we going there?'

Randulph stopped for a moment as they caught sight of the extraordinary building. A John Nash masterpiece the Pavilion boasted domes, towers and minarets in an oriental orgasm of delight.

'It's much better than I expected,' laughed Jane, clapping her hands together with joy.

'Yeah, it's good,' conceded Randulph. 'I had better explain why we are here.'

'Please.'

'OK,' nodded the leprechaun. 'The building has been undergoing extensive repairs for some time.'

'Yes?'

'And they found a photograph in a hidden niche.'

'A photograph. We're here because of a photograph?'

'A very old one, probably a Daguerrotype but before

Daguerre went public with the technique.'

'Surely that's good, isn't it? It must be very valuable.'

'True,' nodded the mage. 'But the subject was extraordinary. It showed George IV entertaining demons in the Royal Pavilion.'

'Demons?'

'That's how you would describe them, I think,' replied the little fellow. 'Though strictly speaking they are probably extra-terrestrial aliens that happen to look to human eyes exactly like demons.'

'Horned devils with red skin, goatee beards, hoofed feet and barbed tails?' queried Jane.

'That's about it,' agreed Randulph. 'Demons.'

'Then they must have been people dressed up or the photograph was somehow doctored.'

'They are much too realistic for costumed actors,' replied Randulph. 'And extensive tests authenticate the photograph.'

'So why are we here? What do we intend doing about it?'

'We are going back to investigate,' stated the mage.

'To the time of George IV?'

'Or before that,' stated Randulph. 'I think that some time between 1815 and 1825 would be about right. We've got to get there when they are first entertaining the demons.'

'Why?'

'We can't allow demons to control the royal family. It wouldn't be right.'

'And you can set up a portal in the Pavilion?'

'That will be no problem as long as we use a part that is original.'

'How can you be sure that we shall arrive at the same time as a demon is present?' asked Jane.

'Didn't I say?' asked the mage. 'In the hidden niche with the early Daguerrotype was a strangely gnarled stone. It was a devil's toenail!'

*

Inside the building Randulph went around tapping various stones, door-frames and floors to the bemusement of the other visitors. Eventually he found what he was looking for.

'The resonance is just right here,' he pronounced, taking out his flute and blowing a few notes.

Immediately Jane could feel the familiar chill, the stilling of the air and then the developing haziness of their surroundings. As the mage played his air on the magic flute the present faded away and the past reappeared.

The room was much smaller and less ornate.

'OK,' surmised Randulph. 'This is slightly earlier than I imagined, nearer to the beginning of the reconstruction.'

'How can you tell?' asked Jane.

'This is the Marine Pavilion which was then redeveloped by Nash,' the leprechaun explained. 'The building started as a farmhouse, was developed into the Marine pavilion and finally Nash created the splendid Royal Pavilion.'

'Where are the demons?' asked Jane in a hushed voice.

Randulph looked around, squinting in the unaccustomed gloom.

'I think they'll be in the next room, don't you?' he indicated towards a slight reddish glow coming from underneath the solid wooden door.

Jane and Randulph moved towards the portal and very slowly opened it, keeping as quiet as possible. In front of them was an extraordinary sight.

'Isn't that King George the Third with his son?' asked Jane.

'David has shown me paintings of them at Windsor Castle.'

'You're right,' answered the leprechaun. 'But look at the creatures with them.'

The demons were huge. Three demons could be seen standing at least ten feet tall their tails stretched out behind them, twitching impatiently and occasionally thrashing from one side to the other.

'Hello, we have visitors!' exclaimed Prince George. 'Look at them, papa, peeping round the door.'

'Oh, oh,' cried Jane. 'They've spotted us!'

'All part of the plan,' grinned Randulph. 'I wanted them to see us.'

'Come in, come in,' ordered the prince. 'I shall introduce you to the king. Your names?'

'Lord Randulph,' stated the leprechaun. 'And this is Lady Jane.'

'Well, well, Randulph and Jane,' demanded the prince. 'Come right inside. Papa, I present Lady Jane and her diminutive companion, Lord Randulph.'

The prince executed an exaggerated bow, his head almost touching the floor and his flesh tight trousers almost popping.

'Ver pleased ter meet yer. Guten abend,' said the king, slurring his words as he did so.

'That's good evening in the German language,' explained Randulph.

'I know that,' hissed Jane in reply.

'Kill them,' cried one of the demons in a deep guttural voice, deeper than any natural voice could reach.

'Righto,' agreed the prince. 'Sorry old beans, seems I have to finish you off. The other members of the Hell Fire and Damnation society have decreed it so.'

'I thought that Hellfire societies has disappeared in the early 18th century?' questioned Jane, whispering in Randulph's ear.

'Speak up,' slurred the king. 'I couldn't hear you.'

'She said that it was her birthday and could we sing to her before she dies?' lied Randulph.

'What should we sing?' asked the prince, a small tear rolling down his left cheek as if he was trying hard to disobey some compunction he was under and the effort was making him very sad. 'I don't know any birthday songs.'

'I can teach you one,' laughed Randulph. 'It's called Happy Birthday.'

'How does it go?' asked the prince. 'Perhaps you and Lady Jane could perform it for us.'

'Certainly,' assented the tiny mage.

He nudged Jane and she responded by joining him in a rousing chorus of Happy Birthday.

Happy birthday to you
Happy birthday to you

Within minutes the king and the prince were joining in singing the banal words. Then they repeated the song.

The demons lifted their heads back, stretched their necks and howled.

'Stop!' cried the evil creatures. 'You must stop!'

But the singing continued and the demons gradually began to fade.

'Now sing For He's a Jolly Good Fellow,' ordered Randulph.

For she's a Jolly Good Fellow,
For she's a Jolly Good Fellow,
For she's a Jolly Good Fellow,
And so say all of us

The words were new to the royal contingent but the tune

was very familiar and they soon joined in. The demons were thrashing in annoyance but faded completely away with a slight popping noise just as the song reached its final lines, second time round.

For she's a jolly good fellow
And so say all of us

For a moment it looked as if the demon aliens were reforming and coming back but Randulph led Jane, the prince and the king in a Christmas chorus.

We wish you a merry Christmas
We wish you a merry Christmas
We wish you a merry Christmas
And a happy New Year

They repeated this several times and then stopped and waited. The demons did not reappear.

'Did you know they were going to do that?' asked Jane.

'Do what?' asked Randulph.

'Disappear if we sang to them.'

'I thought they might,' replied Randulph. 'But it is always good to see that you are right.'

The prince was looking round, wide-eyed and slightly terrified.

'What's been going on?' asked the prince.

'You've been controlled by a mind-seeking parasite from another planet,' answered the little mage. 'But now you are free.'

The king was drooling into his bowl of gruel, his mind clearly deranged beyond repair.

'I believe that contact was made by your Hellfire society and the parasitic aliens have been controlling you ever since,' stated the mage.

'Can you do anything to help my father?' asked a distraught prince.

Jane was trying to speak to the king but was receiving only incomprehensible gibberish in reply.

'Nothing can be done for him,' announced Randulph. 'His mind has gone.'

'But what *is* to be done?' asked the prince. 'He's the king. He is the sovereign ruler of this land!'

'You will have to take over as Prince Regent,' replied Randulph.

'But what shall I tell the courtiers?' asked the prince. 'I can't tell them that we have been in the thrall of demons!'

'Hint that he has had syphilis,' suggested Randulph with a cheeky grin.

'Let people believe that my father had the pox?' the prince was horrified.

'Or some similar condition causing madness,' added Randulph.

'I could, perhaps, imply that it is due to the effect of the moon,' the newly named Prince Regent nodded. 'That might satisfy the curious.'

'Right,' stated Randulph, turning around sharply and taking Jane with him. 'Our job is done. It's back the way we came for us.'

*

They were on a Southern region train heading north, back towards the capital, when Jane asked the obvious questions.

'What is a devil's toenail?'

'It's a fossilised shell of the oyster Gryphaea,' replied Randulph. 'It is one of the commonest fossils found in Britain.'

'So why is it called the Devil's toenail?'

'To quote the Natural History Museum "The robust, curved left valve of Gryphaea , marked with prominent growth bands, superficially resembles a thick toenail."'

'So it did not come from the demons at all?'

'No, absolutely not.'

'Then why did it lead us to the correct time and place?'

'It's the thought that counts not the reality.'

'And are there any mind controlling parasites on our own planet?' asked Jane.

'Plenty,' stated Randulph. 'Hairworms that turn crickets suicidal, wasps that make spiders spin their last web, flukes that make an ant climb to the top of the grass so that they will be eaten and many others.'

'Any that affect human beings?'

'Toxoplasma parasites cause rats to be more bold so they are eaten by cats and the life cycle of the parasite continues.'

'That's rats, what about human beings?'

'It is postulated that toxoplasma may do the same with human beings,' stated Randulph in a lecturing tone. 'And that it may even be a cause of psychotic behaviour. In the past this could perhaps have led human beings into the danger of being eaten by large predators such as lions or tigers. Nowadays it may make us have an excessive liking for the domestic cat.'

'OK,' nodded Jane. 'So mind controlling parasites are not that uncommon and really do exist. But why did the singing make the demons disappear?'

'Ah yes,' mused Randulph. 'It wasn't exactly the singing that did it.'

'So what did do it?'

'It was the repetitive nature of the thought processes involved.'

'So it was because the songs were of a very repetitive nature?'

'That's right. The demonic aliens don't just control minds. They actually feed off intelligent thought and there is precious little of that when human beings are singing their favourite repetitive songs.'

'Would other songs have worked?' asked Jane

'The demons would have disappeared even quicker if we'd sung *Simply Having a Wonderful Christmas Time* by Paul McCartney,' replied the tiny mage.

'Why didn't you get us to do that then?' asked Jane.

'It wouldn't have just left King George III as an imbecile,' answered Randulph. 'It would have damaged all our brains.'

NOTE

I was prompted to write the last story whilst walking around Makro, the wholesalers, and being forced to listen to *Wonderful Christmas Time* by McCartney. The song spoilt my shopping trip but it led to a short story so a big thank you to Macca.

The illustration at the start of the next article is courtesy of Vincent S. Smith [CC BY 2.5 (http://creativecommons.org/licenses/by/2.5)], via Wikimedia Commons.

Keep in shape

Dear Mother/Queen [disambiguation]
I have met a very nice boy. I am keeping myself in shape. I have told him all about myself [dubious/discuss] but I am not sure that he understands. He is teaching me to speak English
Forever with you [verification required]
Sztheanna [translation accuracy estimated at 30%]

*

Dear daughter(s) [edit]
I am delighted that you have found a soul mate [verification required]. I hope that he is compatible. Keep in shape.
Rytheanna [translation accuracy estimated at 30%]

*

Dear Father
I have met the most gorgeous girl. She looks like she comes from Thailand but she is a bit vague about it. She says she is

from the colonies. I am teaching her to speak English with some difficulty. Her own language seems to mostly consist of clicks, rustles and squeaks.

I will bring her to see you as soon as I can.

With love from your son,

David

*

Dear David

Good to hear from you son.

Thailand never was one of the colonies. Perhaps she comes from Burma or Singapore? I thought the only people who spoke in clicks were from somewhere in Africa. Love to meet her,

Your loving Dad.

*

David walked down to his small flat in Bristol thinking that things had certainly looked up since he had met Suzie-Anna, or, as he called her, Suzie or Sue. He was a first year student at the Bristol University studying the Philosophy of Law and he thought that Sue was destined to be his first really significant girlfriend.

He had met Sue when he was illegally racing his car round the 'At Bristol' centre in town. This was the place where the hot rods met up and sported their ware. This was an unusual activity for one of the Law students...it was really the local lads who enjoyed that sort of boy racing but Dave was not too interested in Law. Like many Bristol University students he was fairly wealthy and enjoyed an allowance and the possession of his own car. In his year off after finishing school he had spent some time at a family friend's motor engineering firm that specialised in souping up production cars. This had rather turned him off the Law degree he had registered for and he realised that he enjoyed playing with mechanical objects .....cars in particular.

When he had arrived in Bristol he had brought his own adapted car with him and soon wanted to show it off. Thus it was that he was burning off a local rival in the traffic lights grand prix when he had first met Suzie-Anna.

She had been standing separately from the other girls dressed in a slightly oriental style and not looking at anyone except himself. Realising that she had been noticed she tried to avoid his eye but she did not take much persuasion to go for a spin in his automobile.

David could not help noticing that she enjoyed the trip a lot. In fact every time he had taken her out in the car she had become really excited.

David wasn't quite a virgin but during his other conquests, all two of them, he had been hopelessly drunk and so had the girls. So much so that he could hardly remember whether he had fun or not.

Suzie-Anna was different. She seemed keen to get in bed with him and he just had to find a time when his flat mates were out. Or perhaps she could smuggle him into her own room. He thought she lived in one of the halls of residence on the other side of the Downs but he was not sure. In her broken English, she had described a place with loads of people living together in a community and he reckoned it must be Wills Hall.

She seemed to have a fascination with the stars. He had always enjoyed astronomy and he had brought his telescope with him to University. Perhaps he could entice her into his flat with the suggestion that they look at the stars through the attic dormer window ? Could be fun and he didn't reckon she would take much enticing.

The following Saturday evening the lads and the one girl from the flat had gone out clubbing at ten o'clock leaving David in the flat alone. Sue had agreed to call round at 10.30 to look at the stars but David intended looking at far more than just stellar appearances. He was hoping to get his hands on a heavenly body.

As he waited for Suzie, David felt his pulses racing. Would she turn up or would she just not show ? The anticipation was agony as the minutes ticked past the allotted time.

Trill, Trill.

The telephone rang, not the door bell. Suzie was on the line. She was coming but she had lost her way, could David direct her to the house.

'You are nearly here,' cried David into the phone. 'Take the first left by the Crown and Anchor and its the third house on the right. I'll meet you at the door.'

Within seconds she was there and David was showing her up into his room.

As usual she looked slightly alien in an other-worldly way as she looked round the flat. She hardly ever seemed to take off her sunglasses and this just added to her air of sophistication and mystique but she did seem very excited when David showed her his telescope.

David pointed out the constellations but Suzie did not seem to grasp their significance. She kept saying that the groups of stars he was indicating were really far away from each other and not really grouped at all, something which David was, of course, completely aware.

David showed her his favourite star: Sirius A, a main

sequence star much like the Sun and often called the Dog Star. David liked to imagine a planetary system round the star and life like our own flourishing on a world. He then read out a passage from Homer's Iliad:

> *Sirius rises late in the dark, liquid sky*
> *On summer nights, star of stars,*
> *Orion's Dog they call it, brightest*
> *Of all, but an evil portent, bringing heat*
> *And fevers to suffering humanity.*

Suzie listened intently but had never heard of Homer, the Iliad, Achilles or Troy. She excitedly pointed to a small white dwarf star adjacent to Sirius A, a star that David presumed was Sirius B, and she declared that it was her star. She gave David no explanation for the choice but who was he to argue?

Then he was leading her into his bedroom. He popped into the kitchen to fetch some drinks and when he returned she was already snuggled up in the bed, obviously naked but with the sheet up round her neck and the lights dimmed.

Leaving the drinks on the bedside table, David climbed in next to her. He had kissed her many times before but this was the first time lying down and now he was moving his hands over her warm body. Her skin seemed to quiver at his very touch and she gasped with delight as he snuggled up close to her. He had never felt anything like it before. It felt as if his entire body was on fire, his sensations heightened and his soul absorbed. Sue moved in total concordance with him, massaging him in ways that seemed impossible. Then she let out a strange clicking gasp which obviously meant something in her own language and lay still. Worryingly still to David's viewpoint but after ten minutes or more of complete inertness Sue opened her eyes and smiled in her enigmatic way.

*

Dear Mother/Queen [disambiguation]
I am keeping myself in shape. David has been in conjunction successfully. We shall all be very happy
Forever with you [verification required]
Sztheanna [translation accuracy estimated at 60%]

*

Dear Sztheanna [translation accuracy estimated at 60%]
It is imperative that he was willing. We must not be accused of coercion.
Hold yourself together.
Rytheanna [translation accuracy estimated at 60%]

*

Dear Rytheanna [translation accuracy estimated at 70%]
He was definitely willing
I am still in good shape.
Sztheanna [translation accuracy estimated at 70%]

*

Dear Brother
Have you ever had the crabs. I seem to have caught something.
Must have been from Suzie. Shall I tell her ?
Your worried bro
Dave

*

Dear Dave
I've not had the crabs but my flatmate Pete has. You should go to the Special Clinic (The GUM clinic...genitourinary medicine). They will just get worse otherwise
Steve

*

Dear Bro

False alarm. Nothing to see now even on very, very close inspection (I used Gloria's magnifying glass which she keeps for her stamp collection).

Dave

*

It was a hot summer. Whenever Dave got a chance he would get Suzie to call around to the flat. The other folk in the apartment had got into the habit of clubbing most weekends and even some weekdays so the opportunities increased. There was plenty of fun for Dave and Sue but luckily Dave did not notice any more alarming species on his own personage.

Suzie and Dave also began going out for walks during the day whenever they could.

But David was worried.

As Sue became more fluent in English she seemed to become even more foreign in her way of thinking. It was easy to understand why she made such obvious mistakes when she did not understand a word he said but it was baffling now that she spoke with such precision. And she did indeed speak with such amazing precision. From understanding next to nothing she now spoke English perfectly with an accent identical to his own.

Yes, the mistakes and incidents were strange. Like the time when they were walking on the Downs and they had seen bees swarming in a tree. David had explained that they were dangerously unpredictable. After all it was only the previous summer that a young girl in Bristol had been stung several hundred times by a swarm and had almost died. But Sue had been fascinated by the swarm and had walked right up to them and tried talking with them in her peculiar clicking

language. Naturally they had ignored her completely. Well...
what would you expect ?

Then there was the time when a swallow (or was it a swift?)
had swooped down towards them and Sue had cowered in
David's arms. Or the time when a dog had run up, sniffed her
and run away with its tail between its legs.

There again she seemed to have no idea about Western
culture or government but was very conversant with science.
Surely they would have taught her about history in the
colonies!

She had never heard of Jesus Christ, Julius Caesar, Genghis
Kahn or Winston Churchill or even Buddha or Confucius,
two names she should have known, coming from the Orient.
She did, however, appear to understand quantum theory
and relativity in a way that even his brother, with a Ph D in
Physics, had never seemed to grasp.

David was baffled.

He had also noticed that he was putting on weight.
Everywhere.

His clothes were no longer fitting him as they had. He had
taken to just wearing his pants and track suit but even that
was a bit constricting. Not that he was getting fat and flabby,
just larger and more solid.

Suzie-Anna was definitely not putting on weight. She was
as shapely as ever and twice as beguiling.

He felt that he must find out more about Suzie-Anna before
he took her back to see his father.

Where was she from? He still could not understand her
vagueness.

She always had plenty of time to spend with him. What
was she doing in Bristol ? Was she an illegal immigrant in

England? Could he be accused of harbouring an unlawful alien? That would certainly not help his law career. Did she live in Will's Hall and if not, where did she live?

The Summer progressed and David grew larger, stronger and strangely more clever. In the first year exams David had absolutely no trouble at all. Just one quick read through the relevant chapters the night before and he remembered the lot. David could not help feeling that this was all due to Sue. He began to feel a little uneasy about it all but Suzie-Anna kept turning up as usual, looking cool and collected and dressed in obviously expensive clothes. It was only when you looked really closely that you realised how expensive her clothes must have been. Only haute-couture designers would use such unusual fabric. All of Sue's extensive collection appeared to be made of revolutionary cloth that did not snag, shrugged off liquids and remained clean all day everyday.

A second spell of really hot weather led to disaster.

Rather than stay in the couple had decided to go for a walk in the centre. David was feeling very relaxed and the words of a Creedence Clearwater Revival song came unbidden to his mind.

Oh, Susie Q, Oh, Susie Q
Oh, Susie Q, Baby I love you, Susie Q

Dave could not remember feeling so relaxed and well. He was in this state of mind when a group of youths surrounded the two of them in Broadmead, jeering and wolf whistling as they did so. Three of the group had advanced on Dave and told him to hand over his wallet. Knowing that this was the most sensible thing to do Dave had started to comply but Suzy-Anna had protested. One of the other lads grabbed her and shouted that he would stiff the rich bitch. In a flash a large knife had appeared in the muggers hand and he had stabbed it several times up to its hilt in Suzie's abdomen and chest.

In a rage David grabbed two of the group and to his own amazement lifted them off the ground and threw them several feet through the air.

The other muggers had run away in panic pulling their fallen comrades with them but Sue lay completely still on the ground.

As David looked at her now there was no movement whatever. Strangely he could see no blood from her wounds..... just a thick trail of what looked like lice: small shiny grey blobs moving around independently. Sue was not breathing and he could feel no pulse. He looked around wildly hoping that someone, somewhere would help him. He shouted for help but there was no reply. He remembered his mobile and went to call for the emergency services.

'Don't do it,' came a weak voice.

It was Suzie-Anna calling from the place where she lay on the ground.

'Don't call them,' she croaked. 'I don't want to see them.'

Dave was amazed and relieved to see that Suzie was alive at all. How could anyone have survived the stabbings she had received? Surely with the injuries she had sustained Suzie should have died? The lice-like creatures were no longer apparent and David thought he might have imagined them in the poor light but there was no sign of blood on her surprisingly clean clothes.

The enigmatic Oriental girl was now beginning to get onto her feet so David helped her up.

'We must get away in case they return,' suggested Suzie in a progressively stronger voice. 'I can make it now.'

So saying she began to walk briskly away from the scene of the near fatal attack.

Dave stumbled along behind her. What manner of person was this that she could recover from an assault so quickly and for that matter what was he, himself? He had never had much strength but now was able to throw off several strong assailants.

At the apartment the flat-mates greeted Dave with a smile but went out almost immediately. Dave busied himself making a cup of tea, all the time thinking that it was time to get to the bottom of the mystery. What and who was Suzie? Why was he changing and what was he changing into?

Dave looked at Suzie in a cautious, suspicious way as he carried the teapot to the table. He was worried about her but felt a deep kinship which perfused his whole being. He could not reject her but he had to get some answers.

'Suzie, you must tell me what is going on,' demanded Dave as he sat down heavily on a stout kitchen chair. 'I need to know exactly where you are from, what you are and how you were able to survive that assault. I really thought you were dying.'

'But you know where I'm from,' whispered Sue as she took his hand. Against his will he felt his flesh respond to her touch. 'I'm from the colonies.'

'But which colony,' cried Dave. 'You never tell me. You're too vague.'

'Not from a colony but from the colonies,' answered Sue. 'And as to what am I... well I'm much like you. I am a colony.'

Dave laughed wryly

'What ....Jamaica?'

'No,' said Sue in a hurt voice. 'I thought you understood

what I had been telling you. Not a place but an organisation of living creatures. My cells are intelligent individuals working together in a swarm to create a synergistic whole. I am not one person. I am one colony..... and so are you.'

Dave gasped.

'Are those lice-like animals the creatures you are talking about?'

'They're not really lice,' replied Sue. 'They are collections of my cells that have moved away from the colony and are working independently for some reason. When I was injured they had separated from my "body" accidentally.'

'And when I found then in my pubes they were there purposely?' screamed Dave.

'Of course,' said Sue calmly. 'We had mated and my cells were active on your body.... particularly around your sexual organs.'

'And why do you say I'm a colony?' gasped Dave wildly.

'Because you are and have always have been such,' retorted Suzie. 'Your gut has always been full of bacteria with more individual cells than in the rest of your body, your immune system works intelligently and independently from your brain and each and every cell in your body contains mitochondria .... they also started out as independent organisms.'

'But why have I changed? I'm bigger and stronger than I used to be. Am I suddenly going to burst and an alien crawl out of my belly or will I dissolve into a protoplasmic jelly? What is happening to me? What have you done to me?'

'All that has happened is that we mated just as you wished,' breathed Suzie, still looking exactly like the beautiful Oriental girl that he had first met.

Despite the shocking revelations Dave could still feel

himself attracted to this alien colony. Just as always before his hand went out and stroked her smooth, silken skin. But this time he could not help thinking that underneath the perfect tan was a seething mass of lice.

For some unknown reason the idea no longer disturbed Dave. He felt a pervasive calm and almost welcomed the thought. In fact it only seemed right that she should be a swarm of intelligent cells, after all weren't all higher organisms made of something similar? Shouldn't his own cells work even more intelligently?

In a few moments Dave found himself in bed with Sue pumping away at the same old tingling love pocket.

As they lay still after the love act Dave had to ask more questions.

'You did not really answer my query. What has happened to me?'

'You are now also an intelligent colony made up of self aware cells,' replied Suzie in a matter of fact manner. 'If I cut your skin you wouldn't bleed. A few of the cells, that which you call 'lice', would crawl out and seal the puncture.'

'What has happened to my organs....my heart, my lungs?'

'They are all stronger, self-healing and self-regenerating.'

'And my brain?'

'The same.'

'The same as it was or also stronger, self-healing and self-regenerating?'

'The latter, Dave,' she cuddled up closer to him. 'You wouldn't want your second most important organ to miss out on the upgrade, would you?'

'Am I still me?'

'If you want to be. You are more, not less. You are both you and me.'

'But why and where do you come from?'

'I told you before.... we are from the stars. We have crossed the galaxy searching for partners and you are perfect. Together we make up a perfect symbiosis. You can now live for ever with me.'

'But I'm a freak.... I'm half alien. I'm an outcast from humanity.... a unique liceman.'

'Half alien, yes,' answered Sue quietly. 'But not unique. Once my nucleic acid configured itself so that it was compatible with yours we were able to spread the good deed. In fact you did it yourself every time you touched someone. Haven't you noticed how much nicer your flatmates have been to you? They respect you intrinsically without knowing why. Their new cells are telling them that you are the leader. Number one synergistic colony. As the cells merge more and more you will have increasing control over your mind and body and increasing control over the other human-alien colonies. When they mature, which takes a few days each, they will be able to spread to yet more people.'

'Why did the thugs attack us in the centre?' Dave queried. 'Was that some power struggle between colony clones?'

Sue laughed gently.

'Not at all. They were just evil human youths. But soon they also will be touched by the colonies and become cooperative. They will also acknowledge your preeminence. You are their father, leader and ruler and I am your consort.'

Dave got up slowly and walked over to the window. He looked down to the street level. He thought he saw some of his flatmates outside in the road. They looked up....perhaps they had seen the movement. To Dave's imagination it seemed that they deferentially saluted or perhaps bowed slightly. Then, as he looked, he was certain that they had. A small crowd was gathering and bowing to him. But he still could not forget the lice. Soon the whole population would have been touched by the aliens. They had invaded the Earth without a fight and he was responsible. Should he telephone the police or the army? If he did would they believe him?

And if they did believe him and had not been touched by the lice they might just quarantine the whole area.....or even nuke it!

It would be far safer to keep quiet until everybody had been upgraded.

In any case, he thought to himself with his whole body agreeing. *I'm number one..... She's told me so. She's my Queen.*

It was a lousy world but at least he was the King!

NOTE

Contact with aliens is a very common theme in science fiction. If intelligent aliens did try to contact us it is highly likely that we would not understand them. We find it impossible to converse sensibly with animals on this our own planet despite their biological similarity with ourselves and obvious lack of an extra-solar nature so, as yet, it would have to be the aliens who learn to communicate with us.

And now a story from the world of Jimmy Scott. This tale occurs after *The Witch, the Dragon and the Angel Trilogy* but some time before *Hubble Bubble, Toil and Trouble* (The Witches' Brew).

Faerie Merry Christmas

'Are you sure that you want to go to Faerie?'

Dad asked us this with a sly grin on his face. He knew that we had been angling to take another trip to the alternate reality and that our reply would be yes.

'Of course we do Dad,' we both said together.

You may have heard of our father, Jimmy Scott. No? Well, where have you been for the last couple of years? He is the man who fought the devil, with our help of course. But much of the time he is a normal but rather clever dad.

We live in Redland, Bristol. This is a 'leafy suburb within a short distance of the centre of Bristol', to use the estate agents phrase. We live in a 'well appointed stone-built detached nineteenth century house'.

'Mum should come too,' added Dad and we both nodded in absolute agreement.

I'm Samuel Scott, known as Sam, and I go to Redland Green School. I am twelve years old and I want to be a doctor when I grow up. My brother, Joshua is eighteen years old, has left school and is playing music in his gap year.

It is December and nearly Christmas so the family trip to

Faerie will be an Xmas treat. Great!

Dad wangled a ride in an RAF plane to the Isle of Man. Dad is good at arranging favours like that but then it is not everybody who can fight hordes of demons and hobgoblins.

We were taking off from RAF Brize Norton, just north of Swindon, so we drove there in our old Jaguar. The plane was awesome. A Boeing C-17A Globemaster III: basically a cargo plane but with the ability of taking troops if required to do so.

We were sharing the plane with three Apache sized helicopters. I have always loved helicopters so I asked the RAF staff all about the machines and then about the Globemaster.

Really the plane was on its way to the Falklands but they were dropping us off at the Isle of Man and picking up some RAF bigwig. There were also going to be two other stops before they reached Stanley.

'Lots of scrambled egg I expect,' said the flight lieutenant, an old woman who said she was nearly thirty.

Josh asked what she meant by scrambled egg but I butted in and told him that it was what they called the yellow stitching on the caps of the Air ranks. Josh looked daggers at me for interrupting. He seemed to be staring at the old girl a lot. I think he thought she was good looking but she is ancient compared with him, almost as old as Mum and Dad. But very nice. He even took her email address.

We took off into the wind in a westerly direction and then veered north. The journey took a bit more than an hour and it was raining hard when we arrived in Douglas. An army man, I think he was a sergeant, met us and took us by jeep to the fairy bridge where a small reception was gathered. Dad can't really go anywhere these days without there being local politicians who want to have their picture taken with him.

Dad was very nice to them about it and gave each person from the deputation (that's what he called it) a signed photo of himself, sword in hand. This cheered them up.

Then we went under the fairy bridge and through the gateway into the land of Faerie.

The land on the other side of the inter-reality gateway was very similar to that on the Isle of Man.

'It's not all like this,' said Dad, in case we were disappointed.

'We know, Pop,' replied Josh. 'You've brought us here before.'

'But I can guarantee that you have not been where we are going in Faerie this time,' he answered smartly.

Standing outside the gateway was a huge coppery-gold dragon well over one hundred feet in length, perhaps as much as one hundred and twenty.

'I'm going to be your transport on this part of the trip,' the dragon told us in a lilting female voice. 'We've not met before. I'm Lady Firebrand.'

'Really?' queried Mum, raising her eyebrows. 'I thought that King Clawfang had agreed to take us.'

'He did, Sienna,' agreed the dragon. 'But he is away dealing with an inter-dimensional rift near Alpha Centauri. He'll probably pick you up on your way back.'

'Are you a relative of the King?' asked Mum.

'I'm a cousin and I can assure you that I know the way to your destination.'

I still did not know where we were going but I had a good inkling that it was very connected to Christmas.

'Yes,' said Lady Firebrand, the dragon, reading my mind. 'You are going to the North Pole. You are going to stay at the castle of Father Christmas, known in Faerie as Santa Claus.'

'But we've been to Lapland,' I answered.

'That wasn't real,' protested Josh.

'But this is,' replied Firebrand. 'This is the real home of the real Father Christmas.'

'How can Santa Claus be real?' asked Josh.

'Saint Nicholas is the patron saint of archers, sailors, children and even pawnbrokers,' replied Firebrand. 'And also the patron saint of Amsterdam and Moscow.'

'Yes,' argued Josh. 'But that was the historical Saint Nicholas, a Greek Bishop.'

'This is the home of that very same saint,' replied the elf-dragon. 'He has been living here since your fourth century.'

'How can that work?' Josh was very sceptical.

'Only with huge dollops of Faerie world magic,' replied Firebrand. 'Wait until you meet him.'

Firebrand invited us to climb onto her back. We did so and she took off. There was a strange sensation as we moved through the dimensions......an icy chill down my back and a weird vibration. It seemed as if we were moving through the cosmos and we could see stars and galaxies wheeling in space.

'I thought that it would only be a few miles?' queried Mum in a worried tone.

'It's more than five thousand miles from the place I picked you up,' said Firebrand.

'Why are we going through Space?' asked Mum.

'The quickest route in multiple dimensions is often quite different from the route you would take in the normal three dimensions plus time,' replied the dragon. 'And the route we took was more scenic than plunging through the centre of the globe.'

Mum was rather quiet after that. I don't think she fancied the idea of all of us going through the centre of a planet even if we were protected by a magical force field.

'We're three-quarters of the way there,' announced Lady Firebrand as we slowed down to land. 'Lord James wanted you first to visit the Fairy Castle and a large wyvern will take you the rest of the way.'

I was a little disappointed that Lady Firebrand was not taking us all the way but wyverns are also fun. They are small dragons compared with Lady Firebrand

Standing outside the castle were two animated toy soldiers. They marched over to us and bowed very deeply, bending rigidly at the waist in a very funny way. Dad had told us not to laugh at the fairies but the sight was so funny that I could not help a little giggle. Josh kicked me in the shin and I shut up. It hurt quite a lot!

Lady Firebrand and the soldiers led us towards the castle. The castle was pink and looked as if it was made of icing sugar and put together from several different castles with turrets in impossible places. I thought that I recognised Eilean Donan

but it had lots more bits than it should have done

As I looked at it parts seemed to move around as if jostling to find a better fit but when I got Josh to look at the movement it stopped.

To get to the castle we had to cross a small bridge over a rocky stream.

'Is this the fairy bridge that connects with Skye?' asked Mum.

'It is,' agreed Lady Firebrand.

'Then why couldn't we have come this way rather than via the Isle of Man?' Mum asked.

'The bridge on Earthside is presently undergoing repair,' replied Lady Firebrand, the golden dragon.

She stopped outside the castle and waved goodbye. We all thanked her for her help and she took off into the sky.

Inside we met the tooth fairy who told us that she was the acting ambassador for the King and Queen of the fairies.

'We have prepared a small treat for you!' exclaimed the tooth fairy, clapping her hands.

A dozen fairies suddenly appeared and buzzed round us. They lifted us off our feet and plonked us down in very comfortable chairs that seemed to caress us. Then twenty gnomes appeared and balanced on top of each other. A large brown bear jumped down from a table and started juggling with the gnomes.

'I do hope that none of the gnomes gets hurt,' worried Mum.

'They'll be fine Lady Sienna. Don't you worry,' replied the tooth fairy.

Sure enough they all bounced down again and bowed to us.

Then huge platefuls of food were brought in. This included jelly and ice cream, chocolates and sticky toffee. Also crisps and chips, burgers and chicken legs.

The chicken legs we did not eat! They jumped off the plates and ran out of the door chased by angry gnomes.

'They do that every time,' explained the tooth fairy. 'It's all part of the act.'

We tucked into the food.

'What about the fruit and vegetables?' asked Sienna.

The tooth fairy waved her hands and we could then see that in fact we were eating plates of wholesome vegetables.

'The children prefer to think that it is a treat,' said the tooth fairy. 'But I never actually give them sticky toffee. It's too much work for me.'

I could see that Josh was as infatuated with the fairy as he had been with the RAF flight lieutenant. I preferred Lady Firebrand, the dragon!

When we had finished our food the fairy showed us the fabled talking mirrors. Josh tried to catch them out by asking questions like "What is one divided by zero?"

The mirrors were easily able to answer his problems.

'The answer cannot be defined and is usually denoted as Infinity,' said one mirror.

'A foolish question which deserves no answer,' replied another.

Then it was time to leave the castle and I asked one last question.

'Will we have a good time at the house of Father Christmas?'

'No,' was the curt reply.

'Why not?' I asked worriedly.

'It is his castle not his house,' replied the mirror pedantically.

'OK. But will we have a good time at the castle of Father Christmas?'

I did not hear the reply as Mum shooed me away.

'They're all waiting for us,' she whispered. 'Come along.'

As we trooped out I noticed a furtive looking imp hiding behind a chair. I walked past another of the fabled mirrors and had to ask the looking glass what the imp was doing.

'Come on Sam,' cried Dad. 'We're all waiting.'

'Could you repeat what you said?' I asked the mirror.

'Yes,' replied the looking glass.

I waited but it said nothing then I realised that it was happy because it had answered my question. It could repeat what it had said but clearly was not going to do so unless I asked again. So I repeated the question about the imp.

'You were not listening properly the first time,' replied the mirror in a petulant manner. 'The imp is an assassin that wishes to kill the tooth fairy.'

'Will it succeed?'

'No it will not succeed if you tell the fairy what I have just told you. Twice!' groaned the mirror. 'But yes, if you ignore my information again.'

'Come on,' cried both Mum and Dad.

I scurried out and Dad grabbed my arm.

'Stop!' I cried. 'There is an imp that wants to kill the tooth fairy.'

'How can you possibly know that?' asked Josh in his pretend grown-up voice.

'The mirror told me,' I answered.

'Rubbish,' countered Joshua.

'No!' replied Dad, listening to me intently. 'Did you say a mirror told you?'

'That's right,' I answered. 'I saw the imp and asked the mirror what it was doing hiding in the hall of mirrors. We must help the tooth fairy.'

'This is important,' said Dad, straightening up. 'Soldiers, quick, quick!'

The toy soldiers appeared from round a corner.

'How can we help you, Lord James?' they asked in their soldierly tones. Dad quickly told them what I had learnt from the talking mirror.

'There is no time for delay,' shouted one of the soldiers. 'We must find the tooth fairy immediately.'

We set off in pursuit of the imp and the tooth fairy. We arrived just in the nick of time. The tooth fairy was on the floor with the imp standing over her and it was attempting to pierce the fairy with a long spear. The fairy was caught in a web of some kind but kept twisting and turning away from the spear. The fairy did not look so pretty now and from some angles looked much like a large glowing firefly.

Before the imp could succeed in its evil task Dad whipped out his famous sword and challenged it. The monster turned quickly to take on Dad and enlarged into a creature at least twice the size of Dad and sporting multiple limbs. From one of these limbs it spurted a silk thread that stuck onto Dad's sword arm and pulled him in towards its chomping jaws.

'Enough,' stated one of the soldiers and he bathed the area in a beautiful green light.

Dad and the imp monster stopped still in their tracks. The soldier released Dad's arm and then released him from the spell. The would-be assassin remained completely still and the tooth fairy rose up from the floor, regaining her beautiful appearance.

'Thank you,' said the fairy. 'Thank you both.'

'No problem,' said Dad and the soldier together.

'But how did you know that I was in trouble?' asked the fairy.

'Samuel warned us and insisted we helped,' reported Mum.

'Then I owe my life to your son,' replied the fairy, bowing deeply. 'I shall forever be in his debt.'

She waved her hands around and conjured something from the air. It looked like a small silver bell in the shape of a little Dutch lady with her hands on her hips.

'This bell is magical,' she explained, handing the object to me. 'If you ring it when you are in trouble I will hear it wherever I am and come to your aid.'

'What happens if someone rings it accidentally?' I asked, worried that one of my friends might play with it.

'Don't worry,' she laughed. 'It is attuned to your soul and will only ring for me when you need my help.'

Joshua looked on in amazement as I put the silver bell in my pocket.

'You lucky thing,' he said. 'A real fairy bell. Amazing!'

We were escorted out of the castle in one direction and the scowling imp was led away in the other.

'The imp caught me by surprise,' explained the tooth fairy

as we prepared to board the back of the large wyvern. 'If it had been a straight fight it would not have cornered me. But I really was in trouble so thank you all but especially Samuel. Thank you so much... and keep the bell safe. You will need it.'

The tooth fairy flew over and kissed me right on my left cheek! I knew then that Josh was right. She was truly beautiful and I wanted to pull out all my teeth one by one so that she would come and see me again.

We were on the back of the flying wyvern and the last and shortest part of the journey took a lot longer than the first part. It was exciting flying over the fairy kingdom and we could see many of the famous fairy tales being enacted below us and around us. At one point we flew past a huge beanstalk and the wyvern detoured up into the clouds. There was a castle hidden in the mist and a huge giant was sitting playing a game of Ludo with a small boy, younger than myself.

'That's Jack,' explained Dad.

'Why is he playing Ludo and not fighting the giant?' asked Joshua.

Jack heard the comment and turned round to wave.

'It's our break,' he shouted. 'We'll be back on story in twenty minutes time if you care to wait.'

'No. This is even better,' replied Josh. 'Are you winning?'

'I was but Blunderbore just put two of my counters back to the start,' Jack groaned.

'Never mind,' replied Mum. 'You'll probably get a six next go round.'

'Oh I don't mind,' answered Jack. 'It's the counters. They get very stroppy if they have to go all the way round again. The red ones are the worst. They are liable to get up and walk off the board!'

We started on our way and Blunderbore, the giant, gave us a cheery wave goodbye. Jack had turned his attention back to the board and I could hear his counters muttering and groaning at the indignity of having to begin all over again.

We flew over a family of three bears making their way towards a distant cottage, honey in their paws. We next travelled past the billy goats gruff and a very large troll.

Eventually we left the fairy kingdom at its most northern part and found we were over snow covered mountains. Polar bears and penguins were gambolling together in the clear wintry sun, something I knew to be very odd as they came from different poles on Earth.

In the distance we could see Santa Claus' Castle. It was shining like diamond and sparkling with silver. It was huge and on the top of the highest tower was a big red bell that tolled backwards and forwards, the ringing clearly heard from miles away.

But as we came closer the picture was slightly different. True, the castle shone like diamond but the front gate was barred and there was no welcoming party. The drive up to the castle gates was covered in snow and there were no footprints. The windows had closed wooden shutters and the stable doors had boards nailed across them.

'Strange,' said Dad. 'It wasn't like this last time I was here.'

'That's several years ago,' remarked Mum.

'That's correct, Sienna love,' replied Dad. 'But here it is only a matter of a week or two at the most.'

'How come Dad?' asked Josh.

I knew already so I was not surprised by the answer.

'Time does not work the same here as it does on Earth,' replied my father. 'And at the poles the discrepancy is the greatest. There are just three days here for a whole year on Earth.'

'Christmas Eve, Christmas Day and Boxing Day!' I exclaimed with glee.

'What about the twelve days of Christmas?' asked Josh. 'Shouldn't there be twelve days here for each year on Earth?'

'That's just not how it is set up,' answered Dad. 'With only three days to a year although I came here twenty years ago only 60 days have passed here. About two months.'

'So it is only just over twelve years in Faerie days since Saint Nicholas came here,' calculated Joshua. I was impressed. My brother is very quick at mental arithmetic.

'That's right,' agreed Dad, clearly having done the maths previously. 'But Santa Claus is also a magical figure so even those twelve years should not affect him significantly.'

We had reached the front gate and Dad banged on the boarding. It fell away with a loud clattering of planking. We walked down the frozen track to the drawbridge and reached the portcullis. Again we knocked and eventually a grey-looking elf appeared.

'Can I help you?' asked the elf.

'We have an arranged visit,' explained Dad. 'Lord James Scott and family.'

'Of course,' replied the elf. 'I had completely forgotten. How remiss of me. Did you want to come in?'

Dad looked round back towards the waiting wyvern.

'If we can,' he answered. 'And it looks as if we might be able to help you rather than the other way round.'

I wondered why Dad had said that but the elf led us into the castle.

'There's a problem with Saint Nicholas, isn't there?'

suggested Dad.

'Yes Lord James, there is,' replied the elf. 'How did you know?'

My father did not reply but his look said everything. There was no Christmas inside the castle. No decorations, no tinkling music playing, no elves making toys, no Christmas trees.

'Can we see Santa Claus?' I asked. Josh looked daggers at me but the elf smiled.

'Definitely. He would like that but he probably won't recognise you.'

Dad looked more worried than I expected. How would Santa know me? I'd never met him.

'He normally remembers everyone,' whispered Dad in my ear, obviously noticing my confused expression. 'Especially children. He never forgets children.'

The elf led us along a dirty corridor, festooned with cobwebs. Nobody had cleaned it for a century which was all the more strange if the castle had only been there for twelve years Faerie time.

We then climbed a narrow staircase. The stone steps were worn smooth and curved downwards in the centre due to the wear and tear of passing feet. That would have taken more than one century I guessed.

In a small bedroom at the top of the tower we met Santa Claus. He was propped up in bed with an oddly vacant expression on his ancient face. When he saw us he smiled.

'Hello Nanny Nonna,' he said to Mum. 'When did you get here?'

The elf muttered in my mother's ear and I could only just about hear what he was saying.

'He thinks that every woman is his old Granny,' he explained.

'The poor man has dementia,' replied Mum in her practical nursing tones. 'I can see you are looking after him well but how long has this been going on?'

'It's difficult to say, Ma'am,' replied the elf, looking very worried. 'Time is very strange at the moment here in the castle. It could be a day or a hundred years.'

'Probably happened earlier today,' suggested Dad. 'And I think I know who did it.'

'You don't think this has happened naturally then?' asked Mum.

'No way,' replied Dad. 'We need to get help and quickly.'

'Don't look so upset Papa,' said Santa Claus. 'I'll be better soon. You just wait and see.'

'You will Nicholas. You will,' replied Dad. 'We will come back and see you again very soon.'

'Hello,' answered Santa Claus. 'Who are you? Have you just arrived?'

The elf led us out and back the way we had come. The corridors looked even older and dirtier, the cobwebs thick and choking. Santa Claus' room was the only clean place in the castle.

We went back to the front door and portcullis and looked out to where the wyvern should have been stabled but there was no sign of the beast. The snow was now much deeper and our footprints from earlier had been completely obliterated.

'Where is the wyvern?' Josh asked the elf.

'Goodness me, young sir,' replied the elf. 'The wyvern left years ago. It would have withered away otherwise. We have nothing here to feed it on.'

'What about the reindeers?' asked Josh. 'They must live on

something.'

'I haven't seen any reindeers for a month of Sundays,' replied the elf.

'We need help but how can we get it?' asked Mum.

Then I remembered the bell.

'We could ring for the tooth fairy,' I suggested.

'That is a very good idea,' replied Dad.

I put my hand in my pocket but could not find the bell. I had put it very securely in my inside pocket but it had gone.

'Typical,' groaned Josh. 'You are given something that is useful and you immediately lose it.'

'Now don't argue,' Mum was calming things down. 'The bell must be somewhere.'

'Oh, have you lost a bell?' asked the elf.

I explained about the fairy bell.

'Saint Nicholas has the bell,' replied the elf. 'I saw him playing with it as we left his room.'

'How did he get it from my inside pocket?' I asked.

'He used to be very good at conjuring tricks,' replied the elf, speaking very slowly. 'He used them to entertain the children.'

'Quickly,' countered Dad. 'We must get back up to his room and then you, Sam, must ring the bell. We need help and we need it soon or there will be no Christmas this year, here in Faerie or at home on Earth.'

We ran back along the corridors and up the stairs. The cobwebs were even thicker and the stairs more worn.

Santa was still sat up in bed, holding the silver bell in his right hand and tinkling it next to his ear.

'It's very pretty,' he said with an inane grin. 'Listen everyone.'

He shook the bell again and the sound was very beautiful.

'May I borrow it?' I asked. I did not want to upset the old

man and if I tried to explain that it was really mine I was sure that he would not understand.

'Only for a minute,' agreed Santa. 'Then I must have it back to put on my table with my paper handkerchiefs.'

I took the bell and instantly rang it, hoping beyond hope that the tooth fairy would respond. I knew that she had said she would hear the bell if I was in trouble. Would she also hear it if somebody else was in trouble, not me? In this case it was Santa I was trying to help.

I need not have worried for in a trice the fairy was right there in front of me.

'Have you lost a tooth?' she asked in a worried tone. 'You're a bit big to be losing them now.'

'No,' I replied. 'My teeth are fine but I'm not so sure about Santa's teeth.'

She turned and looked at Saint Nicholas.

'Goodness me!' she exclaimed. 'That's not right. That's not right at all.'

'He has developed dementia,' stated Mum, the ward sister in her taking over again. 'And nobody knows why or how long he has had it.'

'I believe that the imp may have had something to do with it,' added Dad. 'It is too much of a coincidence that the imp should have attacked you on the same day that Santa develops galloping dementia.'

'If it is the same day,' said Josh.

'It is outside the castle,' the fairy assured us. 'But I'm not quite sure how to deal with this development.'

'We could ask the talking mirrors,' I said this without really thinking about it. I was almost surprised to hear myself say it.

'That is an excellent idea,' nodded the fairy. 'I shall call Lady

Firebrand to come to our assistance and return you to the fairy castle where we shall speak to the mirrors.'

The fairy put a cockle shell to her ear and spoke quietly. Within moments the huge dragon was in front of us on the snow.

'I'm sorry that your visit has not gone as planned,' trilled the gentle tones of the dragon. 'But let us see if we can find a way to change things.'

We clambered on the back of the dragon and it instantly teleported all of us to the fairy castle.

'I did not teleport before because I thought that you would enjoy the trans-dimensional journey but speed is of the essence,' she replied to our unspoken question.

We hurried into the hall of mirrors.

'How can we help you?' asked the largest of the mirrors, a hugely ornate bevel-edged mirror within a gold lacquered frame.

'Santa Claus has got dementia. Is there a cure for him?' asked Mum.

'No,' replied the mirror. 'There is no magical cure for dementia.'

We all looked despondent and then I remembered how precise the mirrors could be.

'But is there any treatment?' I asked

'Yes,' replied the mirror. 'In his case there is.'

'And what is that treatment?' Dad asked. 'And how effective will it be?'

'Santa Claus, or more precisely Saint Nicholas, has been cursed by the imp,' said the mirror. 'He has undergone very rapid ageing and developed dementia. A lesser being would have died immediately but Santa's powers are strong.'

'You still have not told us the treatment,' Josh said this rather impatiently.

The mirror turned its attention to Joshua.

'Tut tut,' it said. 'And I was giving you extra information without you having to tease it out of me. So you need to reverse time with a strong anti-chronal spell. The dragon Lady Firebrand can do such spells. That will make the castle come back to life.'

'But what about Santa?' I asked, very worriedly.

'He will need something a bit more subtle,' replied the mirror. 'The best thing would be constant music. I suggest Christmas Carols and Xmas Songs.'

'Will this reverse his dementia?' I enquired.

'Temporarily but since he has the ability to slow time that should be sufficient,' answered the helpful mirror.

'Thank you very much indeed,' I replied and bowed to the mirror. 'And thank you to all the other mirrors who helped me earlier.'

We walked away from the hall of mirrors but I could still hear them chatting to each other. They made my ears burn

'Isn't he adorable?' said one with an attractive female voice. 'I'd do anything for him.'

'You shouldn't really have given that information away without the correct question,' came a pedantic voice talking to the larger mirror. 'But I have to admit that the young lad is a real charmer and it is in a good cause.'

In a matter of moments we were back in the castle. The dragon reversed the spell on the castle and its inhabitants. We went straight up to see Santa and he was still in his bed, lying down with a vacant expression on his face.

'This is where I can help,' said the tooth fairy. 'I am an

amateur musician.'

From nowhere she conjured a guitar and we all started to sing Silent Night.

> *Silent night, holy night*
> *All is calm, all is bright*
> *Round yon Virgin Mother and Child*
> *Holy Infant so tender and mild*
> *Sleep in heavenly peace*
> *Sleep in heavenly peace*

We next sang *Rudolph the Red Nosed Reindeer* followed by *Santa Claus is Coming to Town*.

Santa started to join in then sat bolt upright.

'What has been going on?' he asked in clear authoritative tones.

We explained about the imp and the spell and also mentioned the attack on the tooth fairy.

'I cannot completely halt the effects on me,' stated Santa. 'However the mirror is right and I can slow time. In about a million years from now I may be back in bed again. But now there is work to be done and we are a bit behind schedule.'

He looked at us all.

'The first thing to do is to find proper accommodation for you. You'll be well fed and watered. Then tomorrow, which is Christmas Day, we shall have a glorious time.'

He signalled to a very smartly clad elf, who agreed to take us to our rooms.

'Oh yes,' added Santa Claus. 'Don't forget to take your bell, Samuel.... and thank you for letting me borrow it.'

In a blur he was gone and as we looked out of the window we could see him flying through the air on his sleigh, a huge sack of toys on his shoulder. The sleigh was being pulled by the reindeers: Dasher, Dancer, Prancer, Vixen, Comet, Cupid, Donner, and Blitzen. Leading them all was Rudolph with his nose so bright.

'Ho, ho, ho,' came Santa's echoing laugh. 'Just in time. Just in time! Merry Christmas to everyone!'

NOTE

So, a bit of fun for Christmas time.

And music really does help people with dementia. (http://www.alzheimers.net/2014-07-21/why-music-boosts-brain-activity-in-dementia-patients/)

If you enjoyed that irreverent story you might like to see my videos of the naughty Xmas elf. They are available on my channel on Youtube....just put *Christmas Elf Paul Goddard* into the Youtube search box ..... The first video is *When Santa gets the Sack* and the latest is *Christmas Elf 2014.*

Conclusion

So that was a brief tour round some of my worlds of fiction. I hope you enjoyed the tales. Many more of my stories and poetry can be found via my author's page on Amazon.

(Just search for Paul R Goddard!)

FROM THE REVIEWS OF PAUL'S BOOKS

Witch Way Home?

JJ Mann Amazon
5.0 out of 5 stars A great read from an accomplished author

Liz Varley Amazon
5.0 out of 5 stars An entertaining romp through faerieland with
elves,dragons and Lucifer.
Post apocalyptic making some shrewd points about modern power
politics and politicians.

Tsunami

JJ Mann Amazon
5.0 out of 5 stars. I urge you to read this great book.
Brilliant Gothic tale handled by a true story telling master

Reincarnation

Alien: Amazon
5.0 out of 5 stars: Moved along so quickly that you occasionally had
to take a break to eat....and other things.
I felt sad that it was over.....